The Unfinished Gift

The Unfinished Gift

DAN WALSH

Revell

a division of Baker Publishing Group
Grand Rapids, Michigan

Published by Revell
a division of Baker Publishing Group
P.O. Box 6287, Grand Rapids, MI 49516-6287
www.revellbooks.com

Printed in the United States of America

Library of Congress Cataloging-in-Publication Data
Walsh, Dan, 1957–
     The unfinished gift : a novel / Dan Walsh.
         p.   cm.
     ISBN 978-0-8007-1924-1 (cloth)
     1. Grandfathers—Fiction. 2. Christmas stories. I. Title.
PS3623.A446U54 2009
813'.6—dc22   2009012204

To my children, now grown,
Rebekah and Isaac,

for all the love and joy you have brought into
my life . . . and for all the kindness, mercy, and
patience you've shown me all these years.

I love being your dad.

Acknowledgments

There are lots of people who helped make this book possible, and I do want to thank them. But there are a few whose help was indispensable; without them it would have never made it to print. I will start by thanking them.

First there is Cindi, my lovely wife and First Reader (I don't send anything in that she doesn't like). I'd never have started writing again or kept at it, without her constant encouragement and love. Then there's my mom, who's with the Lord now (but she lived long enough to know this book would be published). She was a great mom and, next to Cindi, my biggest fan. I must add to this short list Mrs. Longnecker (wherever you are), my eleventh grade composition teacher. Her strong encouragement first awakened in me the desire to write fiction.

To my excellent agent, Karen Solem, who believed in me then and now, thanks for all your hard work, guidance, encouragement, and advice. You have made this complex process so easy. To Andrea Doering, my wonderful editor at Revell. First, thanks for saying yes (that was huge). More than that, you are the editor I'd prayed for during all those silent months. Your suggestions and input improved this book, and your friendship has meant the world to Cindi and me.

Now to a few others whose help I simply must acknowledge.

To Michelle Misiak, Carmen Pease, and the whole marketing/publicity team at Revell, for taking a virtual unknown and treating me with such kindness and patience. Also for your creative ideas and hard work getting this book to the shelves. To Cheryl Van Andel and Nate Salciccioli for such an outstanding cover, totally exceeding my expectations.

To Terri Blackstock, for your friendship and advice behind the scenes through the years (what a blessing you have been). To my sister Anne, my typo-hunter, for your love and excellent input. And my other test readers: the Brothers Merwin, Jeff and Tim; and John Morgan (Mr. Prez) for your strong encouragement. And to my beloved friends at Sovereign Grace Church in Port Orange, FL, for all the years and the privilege of serving as your pastor.

And finally, to my Lord and Savior Jesus Christ, whose love and mercy has changed me forever.

One

December 20, 1943

When the black sedan stopped at the traffic light, Patrick rose quietly to his knees in the backseat and peeked out the side window. He flattened his palms against the glass, cold as ice, but he didn't pull back. His eyes were drawn to a large picture window on a house at a nearby corner. Set deep within the night shadows, the window gave the appearance of a painting suspended in midair. Patrick would've given anything to be a part of what he saw inside.

A plump Christmas tree glowed through the curtains. Two stockings dangled from a fireplace mantel. Flames shimmered against the glass ornaments on the tree. A real family, a whole family—mom and dad, two kids, and a dog—sat in a semi-circle around a radio. Probably listening to Christmas music, Patrick thought. Maybe even "Silent Night," his favorite. The mom put her arm around one of the children, a boy about his own age, and tenderly patted him on the shoulder. Tears welled up in Patrick's eyes, escaping down his cheeks. He wiped them away and looked toward the front seat at the rearview mirror, to see if the government lady had been watching.

He had cried more in the last few days than in all his seven short years combined.

He placed his hand on one of the two suitcases beside him. One contained his clothes and a framed picture of his parents hugging, taken before he was born. The other held all the toys he had ever owned and a few picture books. The government lady said he might not be coming back to the apartment for a while. It had something to do with how long it took to find his dad in a place called Europe and whether the army would let his father come home now that his mom had . . .

He couldn't even let the words form in his head.

Instead he thought about his father. He had been gone for a long time, but Patrick still remembered what he looked like. He had studied the picture every night before bed, trying to remember the sound of his voice. It was deep and strong, like the voice of the Shadow. And he was tall with dark wavy hair. He was a pilot on a B-17, dropping bombs on Hitler and all the bad people in Germany so the world could be free. That's what his mother had said. But right now, Patrick didn't care if the world was free. Or if his dad flew bombers or drove a milk truck.

He just wanted him home.

The car started moving again. At the next corner they drove past a Santa Claus ringing a bell beneath a street-light. Next to him, a red kettle. A couple bundled in over-coats walked by. The man dropped a few coins in the kettle and kept going. The Santa yelled "Merry Christmas" in a happy but high-pitched voice. Not a proper Santa voice at all, Patrick thought. "We're almost there now, Patrick," the government lady said. "Isn't it pretty outside with all the lights and decorations?"

"Uh . . . yes," Patrick answered. He knew he should feel that way. He wished he did.

"Do you like Christmastime? It's my favorite time of year."

He could tell she was trying to cheer him up, but it was hard to be in a Christmas mood when your mom suddenly dies in a car crash, leaving you all alone. Patrick noticed her eyes in the rearview mirror. She was looking back. He thought he saw a tear forming, but she quickly turned away. Almost there now, she had said.

Almost where?

He didn't recognize any of these streets or buildings. His grandfather couldn't be a very nice man, he thought. He didn't live very far away. Why had they never visited him? And the way his parents had talked about his grandfather also worried him; they always lowered their voices or changed the subject when Patrick walked into the room.

As the car drove on, Patrick looked at the Christmas lights outlining some of the homes and streetlights. Still, it didn't feel like Christmas inside. Not even the presence of snow lifted his spirits, and Patrick loved the snow.

Almost there, she said.

Patrick felt so lost. They had always lived in that same apartment on Clark Street. This place didn't even resemble his old neighborhood. Everyone here had little yards and driveways with garages. Patrick wasn't even sure they were in Philadelphia anymore. He tried thinking about something happy, starting with the toys he wanted for Christmas. Then he wondered, with everything that happened, would he still get any?

Suddenly a wave of guilt swept over him. He sank low in his seat. Here he was worrying about getting his share of toys, and here his mother was . . . gone. He would never get to spend another Christmas with her. They would never decorate another tree. Sing another Christmas carol. He'd gladly give every toy he ever owned or would ever own again to have her back instead. Even for a day. The tears started coming again.

This time he couldn't make them stop.

Two

The old man's joints creaked in unison with the cellar stairs he ascended. He had just added a shovelful of coal to the furnace. Once upstairs, he glanced at the mantel clock. The boy would be arriving any moment. *The boy.* Just the thought was enough to stir emotions he felt sure had long ago dried out and crusted over. How had it all suddenly become his responsibility? Ida had been gone for many years now, and he'd come to rely on the silence and steadiness of his routines to maintain his fragile peace of mind. What would a little boy mean to all that?

Ian Collins slid his coffee cup under the pot and refilled it to the brim. As he sat at the dining room table, he glanced once around the downstairs of his moderate two-story home. Everything in its place, all as it should be. Even down to the ivory-colored doilies pinned to the armchairs. As neat as if Ida herself were still looking after things. He could just imagine the disheveled state of affairs once the boy got settled in.

Bing Crosby sang "Hark the Herald Angels Sing" in the living room. Nothing but Christmas music on again tonight. The radio carried the only trace of Christmas in the house. No tree. No lights or decorations. That was all Ida's doing.

No reason to keep it up. Collins let out a prolonged sigh. There'd certainly be some pressure applied on him to change that for the boy's sake, him having just experienced such a tragedy. That nosey government woman had already implied as much on the phone, her voice all fake and sweet.

Where is that box of Christmas whatnots, anyway? he wondered. He was sure he hadn't thrown it out. He could still see in his mind a picture of Ida in that last year, two weeks after Christmas, her long gray hair woven tightly in a bun, sitting on the living room floor like a child. She wrapped every item carefully in newspaper and placed them in a big cardboard box, except for the ornaments, which she placed in the exact spots they had occupied in the store cartons.

After her death, when the Salvation Army had stopped by to clear out her things, he had half a mind to let them take the big box along. But he didn't, couldn't. At the time, the feeling came in the form of a posthumous lecture, the worst kind Ida could deliver—eyes only, boring deep within his soul. She would have wanted him to reconcile with their son, Shawn, maybe pass the decorations on to him, like some kind of family heirloom.

No, the box was still in the attic. Had to be. Buried no doubt under a ton of debris, a backache in the making. Well, it could just sit there, he decided. No sense in fussing over it now. If the boy felt the need strong enough, he could sift through it himself in a few days, give him something to do. But Collins would draw the line at a tree. Just no point in it.

He ran his fingers through his thin silver hair and scratched the back of his scalp, then thought he heard the low bass notes of a car engine rumbling out front, then coming to a stop. A moment later, a car door, then another. Had to be them at this hour. He'd better get up before they rang the bell. He had hated the sound of that thing every one of the nineteen years he'd lived there. He lifted his unlit cigar out of the saucer dish and wedged it in between the spaces formerly occupied by his front teeth. Probably shouldn't light it with company almost here, he thought.

He shuffled across the oval rug covering the living room floor. Why'd the boy's mom have to up and die like that? It wasn't a mournful thought, for he truly blamed her for destroying what little relationship existed between him and his son, Shawn. But to leave him alone with the boy like this, even if just for a few weeks. Whatever would they talk about? He'd never said two words to his grandson before, couldn't tell him apart from any number of children playing stickball in the street. And what had Shawn and his wife told the boy about him? About why they had never spent any time together? Probably had made the rift out to be all his doing. That's what they were good at: turning things around so that everything was his fault.

The doorbell rang. He reached down and turned the doorknob, wondering what the purpose of his trip to the cellar had been.

It was still as cold as ice in here.

Three

"Here we are, Patrick. This is your grandfather's street."

Patrick leaned forward in his seat, pressed his nose against the icy window, and imagined which one it might be. She pulled over beside what had to be the darkest house on the street. The lady got out, letting a rush of cold air into the backseat. She had told him her name several times—Miss Townsend. He really should use it when he thought of her; she'd been so nice to him from the start.

He watched her walk carefully along the snow-covered sidewalk, down the driveway, and up a handful of steps until she disappeared within the shadows of the house. Patrick put on his mittens, got out, and stood by the car, his fur-lined cap pulled tight over his ears.

The front door creaked as it opened, like the creepy doors that open on that radio show *Inner Sanctum*. Patrick could see the outlined edges of two adults talking. He took a few steps forward, trying to hear what they said, but kept one hand safely on the rounded fender of the car.

"C'mon, Patrick," Miss Townsend called. "Come meet your grandfather."

He looked toward the backseat.

"Don't worry about your things," she said. "I'll get them in a minute. C'mon."

Patrick walked through the snow, lifting one boot and then another. He tried to stay within Miss Townsend's footsteps, but they were too far apart. Patrick hesitated at the foot of the steps, unsure why.

"Come on, Patrick." Miss Townsend reached down and took hold of his hand.

For a flash Patrick imagined letting his hand slip out of the glove, turning and running back toward the car, then past the car and on down the street. But there was nowhere to go. As he climbed the last stair, he looked up. First into Miss Townsend's face for reassurance, then into the face of a balding old man. An unlit cigar hung down the side of his mouth.

He wasn't smiling.

Ian Collins could hardly believe his eyes. Standing before him, illumined by the dim light, was the face of his son, Shawn, some nineteen years ago. The only difference was the boy's blond hair. From some lost corridor in his mind, he could see Shawn running up those same steps the day he and Ida had bought the house, his face beaming, declaring the house to be as big as a castle. Then Shawn a year later, sitting on the driveway, spinning tops with his friends.

"Mr. Collins?"

"What?"

"Would you like to meet your grandson, Patrick?"

Her words hung in the air with the frosty mist. Collins stood there staring at the boy, laboring to reenter the present.

"Come here, Patrick," the woman said, ignoring Collins's lack of response.

Collins looked at the woman then back at the boy and realized how ill-prepared he was for this moment. The boy walked onto the porch and huddled next to the woman. She put her arm around his shoulder. As he looked up at Collins, Collins discerned a beckoning for approval from the boy but couldn't lay hold of one in his heart. The best he could manage was, "How do you do?"

For a moment, the boy didn't respond. He looked at the woman then back toward the car. "Aren't you going to say hello, Patrick?" she asked.

"Hello," he said. "How do you do?"

"Well, I suppose you brought some things with you," Collins said, looking past them toward the car. "Better see to them, before we let all this cold in the house. Heat barely works as it is."

The woman extended her gloved hand, and a stern expression appeared on her face. "Did I mention my name's Miss Townsend?"

"Pleased to meet you," said Collins, forcing himself to shake her hand. "We can do our talking in the parlor, once we get the boy's things in the house." He stepped back inside, grabbed his overcoat, then walked past them both out to the car. A moment later he stood in the driveway, a suitcase in each hand. "This all?" he yelled.

"Just the two," Miss Townsend replied.

Back in the vestibule, he spread his arms like a mother hen, pushing them toward the front door. As the woman walked through the doorway, Collins noticed that she stopped briefly to inspect his front windows. She shook her head as if disappointed, and he instantly understood why.

It had become every citizen's patriotic duty to hang a little silk flag in the window for loved ones away at war. Most of his neighbors had them. The flags had a red background with a white circle in the center. Within the circle you placed a blue star—making your basic red, white, and blue—one star for each family member in the armed services. Any were killed in action, you replaced the blue star with a gold one. Collins's street had two gold-star mothers thus far in the hostilities. But no flags in Collins's window. No point in putting one up for Shawn, considering the state of affairs. Whatever else he was, he was no hypocrite.

As they stepped inside, the change in temperature was imperceptible, at least to Collins. He set the suitcases by the staircase. "Take your coats?"

"I can't stay," said Miss Townsend. "But Patrick's going to stay awhile, right, Patrick?"

"Can I keep mine on a few minutes? I'm still cold."

Miss Townsend looked at Collins, waiting for him to respond. "I'm sure that would be fine," she said.

They stood there for an awkward moment. Collins finally said, "Right, well, how about I take these upstairs to your room?" He tried hard to sound polite. He turned toward the stairway.

"Before you do, Mr. Collins, may I have a word? I really do have to be going. Patrick, why don't you go in the kitchen? I'm sure your grandfather has some cookies or a nice snack for you." She looked up at Collins, expecting him to affirm.

"I . . . I don't have any cookies." Collins hadn't seen a cookie for maybe a year and a half.

"Do you have any treats?"

Collins thought earnestly then shook his head. "Some fresh liverwurst. I like it with a little mustard on the side."

A look of disgust came over Miss Townsend's face. "Do you have any milk?"

Collins nodded. "About half a quart in the icebox."

"Would you like a nice glass of milk, Patrick?"

"I suppose so."

"Well, you go on and get it. You can drink it at the table there. I just want to talk to your grandfather a minute."

"You're going to say good-bye before you leave."

"'Course I am."

Patrick walked toward the kitchen, looking back at Miss Townsend a half dozen times.

"Make sure you smell it first," Collins yelled to the boy.

As soon as the boy was out of earshot, the woman walked right up to Collins and thrust her face in his. "Mr. Collins, I thought my office had called you about our coming here tonight."

"They did."

"You don't seem very prepared."

"What, because I don't have any cookies for the boy?"

"It's more than cookies."

"What then? I've got a spare room upstairs all ready. Fresh sheets on the bed. Put some extra coal in the furnace."

"That's not what I'm talking about. You know what he's been through. You couldn't even give him a hug?"

"We only just met."

"He's your grandson."

"Listen, Miss—"

"No, you listen." Now the finger started. "I've been with Patrick since just a few hours after the crash. If they'd let me, I'd take him home myself. But with a blood relative so close, the law says he comes to you. He is a sweet, sensitive boy. With all he's been through, he's hardly complained at all. We're doing everything we can to get his father back, but he's going to need someone to help him cope until then."

"Young lady," Collins said, taking a step back, "I'm not accustomed to being lectured in my own home. I think it's time for you to leave."

She got a certain look on her face. If Collins discerned correctly, she wasn't far from giving him a good slap.

After a long, silent moment, she said, "It *is* time for me to leave. But I want to remind you: I am responsible to the state for Patrick's welfare until he's reunited with his father."

"Your point being?"

"I am authorized to stop in from time to time to check on him, and, mind you, I don't have to call first."

"The boy's got nothing to fear from me."

"The boy? You can't even bring yourself to call him your grandson? Or at least his first name?"

Collins walked past her toward the front door. "You did say you were leaving."

She shot him a hateful look, then called out, "Patrick, come here a minute. I have to go now."

A glass rattled in the sink. "You haven't mentioned anything about the boy going to school," said Collins. "Shouldn't he be in school at his age?"

"He's in second grade, if you're really interested. But we've decided it's best not to send him just now."

"Why?"

"It's only another day or so before they're out for the Christmas break," she said, "and you live in a different district. With all he's been through, it just doesn't make any sense."

"I think you're making a mistake," Collins whispered, noticing Patrick walking through the dining room in their direction. "He'd be much happier around children his own age."

Miss Townsend paused, then whispered, "You're just trying to get rid of him, aren't you? You can't bear the thought of spending time alone with him."

What an insolent woman, Collins thought, returning her hateful stare. But what she said was true. Still, she had no right to say it.

Patrick ran the last several feet straight into Miss Townsend's arms. "Sorry," he said, pulling back.

"No, that's all right." She drew him back to her embrace, a tear rising in her eye. She bent down on her knees and looked directly into his face. "Let me see that smile. That's better. Now, you remember, Patrick, I gave you my card. It's right there in the side pocket of your coat. My office number is on the front, and I even wrote my home number on the back. If you need to call me for any reason, day or night, just call. You don't even need your grandfather's permission." She looked up at Collins's sour expression. Patrick started to look also, but Miss Townsend gently redirected his face back toward hers. "I promise you, I will do everything in my power to get your father back here as soon as we can. Do you understand me? Everything I can."

At that, Patrick collapsed into her arms again and began to cry.

Yes, please bring Shawn home quickly to get his boy, thought Collins. At least on that point, he and the woman could agree.

Four

After Miss Townsend had gone, Patrick felt very alone. This wasn't at all like being with a grandfather. Not from what he had seen in the movies. And he'd seen his friend Billy's grandfather a number of times. He called his grandfather Pop-Pop. The first time Patrick heard it, he laughed out loud. But after his third visit, Pop-Pop seemed just about right. Patrick didn't even know what to call this man. So far, he just called him "sir," and the man hadn't corrected him.

Patrick heard Miss Townsend's car starting out in the driveway. The old man picked up his two suitcases and started up the stairs. "Follow me," he said. "But first, hang that coat on the closet knob there. It's the door at the foot of the stairs. And you'll probably want to drape those mittens across the radiator, else they'll still be wet come morning."

The lights were out at the top of the stairs, so Patrick didn't get a good look around. The man walked straight ahead across the slippery wooden floor and turned a light on inside a tiny bedroom. The whole upstairs smelled funny, like lavender soap. He set Patrick's two suitcases down on the bed.

"You got pajamas in there?"

"Yes, sir," Patrick answered. "I can get them."

"Well, let me show you the bathroom first. Now, don't go turning on a lot of lights up here if you need to get up at night, like that hallway light. You only got a few steps to walk in the dark to reach the bathroom. Here, let me show you."

He walked Patrick out into the dark hall. The light shining from Patrick's room revealed three other doors, all closed. The stairs were straight across from his doorway.

The man opened the third door and said, "Now, don't go opening this door, see. At least, not at night. And in the daytime, you ask me first. It goes to the attic. There's no light switch but at the top of the stairs. You go trying to find your way up here at night and you'll break your neck." He opened the second door. "Here's the bathroom. You need to use it at night, you just walk right across the hall in this direction. See, you don't need to turn on that hall light, do you?"

"No, sir, I can see it." Patrick knew instantly where the smell of lavender soap was coming from. He could probably find the bathroom at night just following the scent.

"This third door goes to my room. Right, well, I expect you'll be needing to wash your hands and brush your teeth before you turn in. You need help with that?"

"I don't think so."

"Now, don't go using the soap in that box there," the man said, pointing to the back of the toilet at a fancy box labeled "Cashmere Bouquet." "You see it?"

Patrick nodded.

"That's too dear, so don't go washing your hands with it. Use the soap by the basin."

Patrick looked carefully at an orange, egg-shaped blob centered in a metal tray, soaking in a shallow puddle of sink water.

"Right, well, I better get downstairs and clean up a bit before I turn in. You'll be all right up here?"

Patrick said yes, but he wasn't sure at all. The man backed out of the bathroom, turned out the light, and walked down the stairs. No kiss good night. No hug. He didn't even say good night. The whole upstairs suddenly felt very dark and cold.

Patrick walked back to his bedroom and looked inside. A small bed was shoved up into the right corner. A window covered in blinds occupied the left corner, and beneath it, a radiator. Just inside the door sat a three-drawer dresser with a white doily on top and some kind of picture frame. Patrick made a special note to memorize the location of the light switch.

Darkness was, and always had been, his mortal enemy.

He closed the bedroom door and opened the larger of his two suitcases. He lifted his mom and dad's picture out and carefully set it on the dresser. He tried to imagine them being there with him instead of so very far away. He imagined them telling him good night and not to worry about his grandfather being so unkind. His mom spoke first. He was glad he could remember her voice so strongly.

"Patrick, I'm in heaven. You know that, don't you?" She used the soothing tone she always used just before bed. "I'm not in that coffin they buried in the ground. I'm with Jesus and the angels. And you know what? Jesus told me he's assigned a very special angel to watch over you and keep you safe." His mom had often read him Bible stories before bed. He remembered the night she read him Jesus's words about children having special angels to look after them. A few days later, he had seen a picture in a magazine of some famous painting filled with angels. Some were just little babies with tiny wings and their rear ends sticking out. But there was one in the center who looked like a mighty warrior with a sword raised high toward God's throne. Patrick showed the magazine to his mom right away. She had assured him that his angel looked more like the warrior than one of those pudgy babies.

A tear formed in his right eye as he remembered the moment, so he looked at his father's face. His voice was a little harder to imagine. "Patrick, I know you don't know my dad, but he won't hurt you. I promise. If he does, I'll punch him in the nose when I get back. Even if he is my dad." Patrick laughed at that. He wasn't sure his father would say that, but he liked it just the same. "I'm still over here fighting the Nazis," he continued, "but I'll come get you real soon. I promise."

Patrick sighed. This helped a little. But he wished so badly his father could be there now. He turned and carefully lifted his pajamas from the suitcase. After putting them on, he was able to pull the smaller suitcase to the floor; the larger one was too heavy. He could only slide it toward the foot of the bed. He walked over and flipped the light switch, instantly plunging him into a terrifying darkness. He ran for the bed and hopped in, wrestling the bedcovers from under the suitcase.

He lay shivering in fear for several minutes until his eyes adjusted, aided by thin rays of light seeping in from the blinds. The moon, he thought. His mother had told him stories about the moon, how God had made the moon to guide us at night, how sailors and great adventurers used the moonlight to find their way in times of trouble. He quietly got out of bed and stepped to the window. He fumbled in the dark for the strings then slowly slid the blinds up. The sight of a full moon hanging suspended in the sky brought some relief from his fears. And it was warm leaning up against the radiator.

For a few moments he just stared up. "Can you see me

here, God?" he finally said, looking right at the moon. "I'm not where I usually am. But Mom said you're smarter than a million men, and you can see everything all at once. Can you see my mom sitting there next to you? She'll probably be in a chair; she doesn't sit on the floor. Her name is Elizabeth . . . but you know that, because you know everything. I can't remember if it's okay to talk directly to her or not. I think she said we're not supposed to talk to anyone in heaven but you." Looking at the moon made it easier to believe God could really hear him.

"Please tell her I miss her, and that I'm with my grandfather . . . the one we never visited. I don't know what she'll think of that, but I had to go where Miss Townsend said. Tell her . . ." He started feeling a deep sadness thinking about her being way up there in the sky. He knew if he didn't end this prayer quick, he'd start crying all over again. "Tell her I love her, and I'm trying to remember everything she taught me." The tears started to fall. "I can't talk about her anymore." He wiped the tears away with his sleeve. "I just have one more thing. It's maybe the most important favor I ever asked you."

He looked around his small room, what he could see of it in the moonlight. It wasn't his room. It was just a bed, a dresser, an empty closet. A closed door. A cold world beyond that. "Please bring my father home from the war," he said. "Please let it be quick like Miss Townsend said. Don't leave me here alone. Please don't leave me alone."

He stumbled into his bed, crying as quietly as he could, looking up toward the light coming in from the window. He cried right through until his mind gave way to sleep.

Across the Atlantic, along the peaceful East Anglian countryside, sleepy cows grazed along rolling hills. Small herds of sheep fed in rich pastures bordered by ancient stone walls and hedgerows. Narrow country lanes weaved their way up and down and through the serenity, splitting the scene from the sky up above like the seams of a patchwork quilt. But this morning, the placid scene could not be observed from the sky above, except by God and his angels. The notorious English fog had made the simple act of putting one foot in front of the other a perilous business.

For the last two hours, it had grounded the 91st Bomb Group, now stranded along the taxiways of Bassingbourn airfield. In dozens of B-17 Flying Fortresses, young men sat braced for action, silently hoping the fog would remain, guaranteeing them at least one more day on the planet.

In the cockpit of one such B-17 sat Captain Shawn Collins, Patrick's father.

Several days ago, the telegram carrying the tragic news of his wife Elizabeth's death had reached the Eighth Air Force headquarters, twenty minutes west of London. But it did not reach Bassingbourn airfield in time to keep Captain Shawn Collins off the roster for the next bombing mission.

An air raid to Bremen, deep in the heart of Nazi Germany.

Five

A poached egg, cooked for exactly two minutes. Any more and the yolk gets hard; any less, the whites get runny. A little salt on the egg, a dash of pepper. A piece of dry toast to put it on. Before the war, he liked it buttered. A cup of coffee, black.

This was Ian Collins's breakfast routine.

The only variety was the occasional glass of fresh tomato juice presented by Mrs. Fortini, a widow who lived next door, from tomatoes picked from her Victory Garden out back. Hadn't seen much of that since winter began, but what she used to bring over was generally quite good. Then again, she was Italian; her people were good with tomatoes.

The sun wasn't up yet. Out toward the street he heard the usual commotion that occurred every weekday about this time. A steady stream of strangers making their way down the road toward the bus stop. In fifteen minutes a bus would haul them off to the Carlyle tank-manufacturing plant at the edge of town. Young women and elderly men, for the most part. Collins could have joined them if he had a mind to, but he didn't need the money and sure didn't prefer the company.

Before the war he had owned a small machine shop and dabbled in a little engineering on the side. Got a couple of patents for this widget and that, mostly tank parts he sold to Carlyle. When Ida had taken ill, he decided to sell the shop off, since Shawn was too foolish to see its potential.

At the time, Carlyle Manufacturing had just gotten a handful of contracts from England to build assemblies for a new breed of tanks for the Brits. Carlyle needed all the machining equipment they could find, but they had a cash-flow problem. Collins settled the deal by accepting a cash down payment for the shop and a small percentage of their business for the balance. Best decision he'd ever made. With the escalation of hostilities, Carlyle's business had grown tenfold since then and was still climbing. Collins had made so much cash, he finally had to break down and deposit most of it in the bank.

Except for his lawyer and banker, no one knew anything had changed. Not even Shawn. The only luxury the elder Collins indulged was upgrading to Cuban cigars.

He sat at the kitchen table and ate his first bite of his egg-on-toast when he heard a loud noise out by the street. Sounded like someone colliding with a trash can. Somebody else laughed followed by someone else telling them to be quiet. They had better not wake up the boy, Collins thought. This was the only peace and quiet he expected to get this day. He grabbed his cup of coffee and made his way through the living room.

He set his coffee on the sill, put on his coat and fur-lined cap, still wearing his pajamas. He would just stand on the porch a few moments, glaring at the workers as they passed by. That would usually quiet them down.

This, too, had become part of his morning routine.

∽

Patrick awoke confused. An unsettling dream had placed him back in time with his mom, standing outside Sanders Grocery at the end of their block on Clark Street. She had just gone in to pick up a string of breakfast sausages. He stood outside, watching as the street and sidewalk filled with shoppers going about their day, trying to sidestep puddles left from a morning rain. A poster hung in the front window of Sanders's store, urging everyone to buy more war bonds. Some older boys had just passed by escorting a pony straining under the weight of a teetering cart full of scrap paper and metal.

As Patrick waited outside, it dawned on him that she was taking too long. Something was wrong. His mom had said to wait right there, but he couldn't wait anymore.

He walked into the store, expecting to find Mr. Sanders behind the counter helping a row of customers, but the store was empty. Patrick walked past each of the four narrow rows of canned goods. They were empty too.

"Mom?" he cried out. "Mr. Sanders? You in here?" He stood still, listening. No one answered. He walked behind the counter, forbidden territory, hoping to find someone stocking the lower shelves, but the counter aisle was empty too. "Mom?" he yelled, panic rising in his voice. His face felt hot. He walked through a doorway leading to the back room and peeked inside.

No one there.

Tears rolled down his cheeks. He ran through the store again, hoping somehow he'd missed her on the first pass. But there wasn't a soul inside. "Mom?" he cried again as he ran out the front door. "Where are you?"

He froze. Now the entire street was empty. No people or cars, horses or trolleys. "Mom!" he screamed. "Where are you?" He put his hands to the sides of his mouth and yelled at the top of his lungs: "Where is everybody!"

Then he woke up.

The sick, scary feeling still hung in the darkened room for several moments as his eyes adjusted to the morning light. Then he remembered where he was.

Reality brought no comfort.

He sat up slowly, trying to focus on his mom and dad's picture. This morning, they seemed stuck inside the frame, unable to speak. He grabbed his pillow and gave it a tight squeeze. Sometimes when he did, he could imagine it was his mom; sometimes she even hugged back. This morning it was just a pillow.

He really was all alone.

Six

Later that morning, Patrick sat eating a bowl of oatmeal at the dining room table when he heard a loud knock at the door.

"I'll see to that," Ian Collins said as he walked toward the front door. "You finish up there, and don't forget to rinse the bowl in the sink. Stuff hardens like mortar."

Collins got on his toes and peeked through the center window in the front door. *Geez*, he thought, *not now*. It was Father O'Malley from St. Joseph's a few blocks away, standing in his vestibule, nose and cheeks bright red from his short walk. It was bad enough Collins had to sit through one of his monotonous homilies every Sunday at mass; now the man was at his front door. Collins tucked in his shirt, worked out a kink in his neck, and turned the knob.

"Marnin' to you, Ian," Father O'Malley yelled through the glass door, his Irish brogue strong as the first day he set foot in America just after the Great War. His black hat was pressed down over his ears and his hands shoved deep into the recesses of his black overcoat.

Collins quickly opened the door, noticing the sun was shining brightly now. Small wet clumps of snow fell from the father's shoes as he banged them on the steps. "I'm sorry you had to walk through that, Father. I'd hired a boy to come shovel the walks for me, but he never showed up."

"Quite all right, Ian. Good help's hard to find these days."

The two men walked into the living room. Collins quickly closed the door. He tried to remember the last time Father O'Malley had stopped by. Seemed like it was just after Ida had passed away.

"Is that the boy?" Father O'Malley whispered, looking Patrick's way.

How did he know about Patrick? Collins wondered if the good father might be more connected to the Almighty than his sermons gave evidence.

"'Tis such a shame," said the priest. "To be so young and without your mother."

He took off his coat and handed it to Collins, then his black leather gloves. *Guess he plans to stay awhile*, Collins thought, trying to restrain a sigh.

"I lost me own ma when I was a lad, but I was eleven at the time." The priest walked over to the radiator and warmed his hands. "He can't be, what . . . seven or eight?"

"Seven," Collins whispered. He looked at Patrick, making sure he wasn't overhearing the conversation. The boy's eyes seemed transfixed on the back label of the oatmeal box. "Can I get you something to drink? Coffee? Got half a fresh pot left."

"That'd be nice. It stays this cold and we might have ourselves a white Christmas, just like the song."

Father O'Malley looked about the living room, noticing the absence of Christmas, no doubt. Collins hoped he didn't bring it up; he wasn't in the mood for another lecture. "Well, let me get you that coffee, Father." Anything to change the subject. "You take cream and sugar?"

"You have sugar?"

"Enough for coffee."

"Just a teaspoon, then. No cream."

As Collins turned toward the dining room, Patrick was standing in the doorway, eyeing them both with an unsettled look.

"Now there's a handsome lad," said Father O'Malley. "Come over here. Let me take a look at you."

Patrick looked at Collins for permission. Collins nodded.

"Why, he's the spitting image of Shawn, Ian. Don't you think? An amazing resemblance."

Collins shot him a menacing look. Not intentional. He was grateful the priest didn't seem to notice. He seemed mesmerized by the boy.

"What a smile you have." Patrick stood in front of him, the priest's hands resting on his shoulders. "Aren't you a bit tall for a seven-year-old?" Patrick smiled even wider at that. "I knew your father when he was a boy. Did you know that? A little older than you are now, but you look just like him. Tell me, what's your name?"

"Patrick."

"A fine Irish name. Your father was quite the baseball player. Helped St. Joe's win the city championship when he was in high school. You like baseball, Patrick?"

Patrick nodded.

Collins figured the boy could find little trouble spending time with a priest, so he attended to the coffee. As he poured, he noticed the boy's oatmeal bowl had not only been rinsed but washed and set upside down on the draining board to dry. When he returned, Patrick was sitting next to Father O'Malley on the davenport. Collins set the priest's cup on the table in front of him and sat down in his favorite chair.

"The lad's just asked me an interesting question, Ian. I

wonder if you can answer it for the both of us? He wondered if Catholics celebrated Christmas. Noticed there aren't any Christmas decorations in the house, no stockings, not even a tree. What do you make of that?"

Collins panned the room, hoping an explanation might surface to forestall the sermon he knew was coming. "I've been rather busy lately" was all he could think to say. This was setting up to be a miserable morning. Collins had always felt that having to consider one's religion an hour each Sunday was more than sufficient.

"But Ian," the priest said, "I'm looking around and I don't see any signs of Christmas at all in here. Aren't you planning on celebrating the birth of our Savior?"

Collins sighed. "I do . . . in my own way."

"Miss Townsend told me, from what she gathered, that Patrick's mother was a very strong Christian. I'm assuming she raised Patrick the same. Isn't that right, son? You'll be wanting to celebrate Christmas, won't you?"

Patrick nodded, then cast a worried look at Collins.

"Miss Townsend," Collins said. "She tell you to come over here?"

"No. She did call briefly, but just to inform me of the boy's situation."

At that, Patrick stood up. "May I be excused, sir?" he asked Collins.

Collins did not immediately respond; he was trying to diffuse the anger in his heart.

"It probably would be best if we didn't discuss these matters in front of the boy," Father O'Malley said.

It'd be better if we didn't discuss them at all, Collins thought.

"Isn't there a pleasant task we can give him to do, Ian? How about Christmas decorations? Would you be having any decorations he could sort out, bring this house into the holiday season?"

Patrick's eyes brightened at the notion.

"I suppose it wouldn't do any harm," said Collins. "But I'm going to have to take him up in the attic. Ida put a big box up there full of the stuff."

"You see, Patrick. Catholics celebrate Christmas. You should see the way we've decorated the church . . . and the rectory."

"What's a rectory?" Patrick asked.

"It's a place where priests live."

"You just finish your coffee there, Father. I'll be down in a few minutes. C'mon, Patrick. Let's go find that box."

Collins walked up the stairs, the boy right behind him. As he walked past the boy's bedroom, he noticed the bed was made, with almost perfect military trim.

Seven

Patrick had only been in one other attic before. It had been a wonderful experience, ranking up there somewhere between the toy store and candy shop. He followed closely on his grandfather's heels. The steps were steep and narrow, so he pretended he was climbing the face of a cliff.

"Mind yourself, now," his grandfather said. "I'll get this light on in a minute. Stupid fool thing putting the switch at the top of the stairs."

When they reached the top, his grandfather opened the door. It was just as Patrick had imagined. At first it was dark, but his eyes soon adjusted. Boxes of every shape and size came into view, overflowing with bounty, like pirates' treasure. Every metallic object sparkled from bright rays of sun pouring in from two dormers. It was like a page out of a storybook. Collins shuffled away from the stairs toward the front of the house. Patrick had stopped following, mesmerized by the scene.

Collins turned and snapped, "Now, don't go getting any ideas. You go messing around, something's liable to come down on your head, get that government lady all over me.

Get over here and stick by me. Only one box up here we're after."

Patrick sighed. The adventure was over. His mother had never yelled at him like that. Not once in his entire life. There was just enough room to walk in between the boxes if he turned sideways. He obeyed and soon stood a few feet behind his grandfather.

"Where'd I put that stupid thing?" Collins said. He started lifting boxes, putting them here and there, setting off little dust explosions.

Patrick wondered how anyone could call a box of Christmas decorations a stupid thing. Collins continued muttering as he searched. It was hard for Patrick not to let his attention drift, but he didn't want to get yelled at again. Every now and then, he moved one of the boxes Collins set near him an extra inch to the left or right, just to make a contribution.

"Don't touch," Collins snapped. "You trying to knock something over?"

"I'm sorry."

"Just leave everything alone." Collins turned back toward the boxes.

Patrick bit his lip. Tears wanted to come, but he wouldn't let them.

"Just stand over there if you can't keep your hands off things."

"I won't touch anything again, I promise."

Collins turned back around. "Where is that box?"

Patrick stepped back into the shadows; even a few feet felt safer. His eyes wandered around the room. He quickly noticed an army uniform hanging on a rack next to an oval dressing mirror. A real army uniform. Was it his grandfather's? His dad wore one just like it. He remembered him standing at the train station, a thousand people pushing and shoving, crying and hugging good-bye. Then it was time for his dad to say good-bye. His mom was crying, and then he was too. His dad picked him up, high in the air. "You're in charge, Patrick. You take good care of Mommy till I get back, okay?" But he hadn't taken good care of Mommy, had he? His dad had given him just one thing to do, and he couldn't even do it.

"There it is, son-of-a-gun."

Patrick turned back toward his grandfather, glad for the distraction.

"Had to be under ten other boxes." He groaned as he pulled the box free. "Yep. There's Ida's writing. You could spell better than her. Look at that . . . orma-nents . . . Christmas orma-nents."

He was smiling, the first time Patrick had seen him smile. Billy's grandfather always smiled, even gave horsey rides and told knock-knock jokes.

"Okay, Patrick. Come here."

His grandfather had just pried the box lids loose and bent them back. Patrick looked inside and saw . . . Christmas. A bright gold star lay on top. Boxes of shiny glass ornaments were stacked around the sides. He saw the roof of a nativity scene, with wooden characters lying on top and inside, some wrapped in tissue paper. There were at least a dozen ceramic figurines: snowmen, carolers, Santas, and elves.

"I've got to go back down and see the father for a few minutes. Can I trust you alone up here?"

Patrick nodded.

"Take a good look inside this box before you touch any-thing. When you leave this house, I want everything put back just the way you see it here. You hear? You can leave any tree decorations alone. We're not setting up any tree. I expect your daddy to be home in a few days. Plenty of time to get you a tree. Just pick out a few things to put around the living room or your bedroom. You understand?"

"Yes, sir."

"All right, then. I'm headed back down. Mind yourself coming back down the stairs. Don't bother with the light switch. I'll come back and turn it off later when you're through." Collins stood up and made his way back to the attic stairs.

Patrick didn't move until he heard him get all the way down. When the attic door closed, the room was suddenly alive again. He looked inside the Christmas box. It shouldn't be too hard remembering where things went. All the ornaments were in boxes stacked along the sides. He carefully lifted out the big golden star and looked for a safe place to lay it down.

That's when he first saw it.

On the far side of the room, just beside the army uniform . . . it was leaning up against an oval mirror. This big wooden soldier. Years later, Patrick would still remember the first moment he laid eyes on it. Everything else in the room had suddenly gone out of focus. There was only the wooden soldier. It was hand carved, maybe eighteen inches tall. Unpainted, made of some light-colored wood, and finely detailed. It looked like a soldier from World War I, wearing one of those old pie-panned helmets. The expression on his face was stern, like he was yelling something at the top of his lungs. His rifle was fixed upward, as though storming a hill, his bayonet pointing at some invisible enemy.

For a few moments, Patrick stood frozen in place. A warning began to form about what his grandfather would say if he got distracted from his main goal. But the warning was quickly overcome by the power of curiosity and desire. He stepped carefully through the maze of boxes and narrow aisles, his eyes fixed on the soldier. He couldn't imagine the awful consequences if he knocked anything over along the way.

Finally, a clear path opened. He picked it up gently, glad to find it was sturdy and well made. He noticed the bottom was unfinished, the legs blending into a block of wood. Who could have taken an ordinary block of wood and turned it into such a thing of wonder?

He held it at arms' length and instantly decided that he had never wanted anything so much as this wooden soldier. The look on its face was so fierce, so intense; he could feel the soldier's courage, see the bravery etched in every line. Patrick had seen newsreels about World War I and wondered what it must be like to face such danger, bombs going off to the left and right, machine guns rattling all around you. Yet still you run out of the trench to face it all. In the films you could never see the soldiers' faces.

But now he could.

And it was the most remarkable thing he had ever seen.

Eight

After securing the boy in the attic, Collins spent some time in the bathroom, taking a bit longer than usual. He thought about staying upstairs even longer, maybe ten minutes more. If the priest stayed, Collins could just say the box had been difficult to find. Or Father O'Malley might get antsy and have to leave. Then came an image of Ida, like a fierce look from heaven for treating a holy man so poorly. He washed his hands and headed back down the stairs.

For the next fifteen minutes, the father asked a lot of questions about Shawn. How could Collins tell the father he hadn't talked to Shawn since before the boy was born? What new avalanche of words might that rain down upon him? As he talked, Collins drifted back to the last conversation he'd had with Shawn.

It, too, had been about issues of faith. Shawn was even sitting in the same seat as Father O'Malley. Shawn had been trying to persuade Collins into considering how much more God had in mind for his life, what real faith in God looked like. Went on talking about how Elizabeth had helped him understand so much more about the gospel. Imagine the nerve, a son talking like that to his father.

"Dad," Shawn pleaded, "please just listen to what I'm trying to say, just for once." Then came this look of frustration, or was it disgust. "Who am I kidding? You've never listened to me, have you? It's always been about me doing things your way. Well, it won't happen this time, it can't happen. The stakes are too high."

"What kind of nonsense is that?" Collins shot back. "Always doing things my way," he repeated. "As I recall, you're not following me into the shop every day, even though this whole business could be yours in a few years. Got your way on that. Joined this new Army Air Force instead of the infantry like every other Collins who's ever fought for his country. Got your way on that. And now you've up and married a woman who's not even Irish and talks about religion all the time, totally against my wishes. So, maybe you can help me see how it's always got to be about my way."

Shawn stood up, a full four inches taller than his father, and paced in front of the coffee table. When he spoke again, he seemed a little more in control. "Okay, Dad, you're right. I did get my way on those things. But you're missing the point. I'm not a child. I shouldn't have to fight for my way on things like that anymore. Each of those decisions was mine to make, not yours. Did you make it easy for me to make any of those choices? Did you even try to understand a single one? No, you did everything in your power to shut me down before you even heard me out."

Collins didn't reply.

"You seem to think every time I disagree with you, I do so out of spite," Shawn said.

"I say black, you say white," said the elder Collins. "I say up, you say down."

"That's not the way it is."

"It's exactly the way it is," Collins shouted. "At least for the last two years. Ever since you met—"

"It is not. Look . . . I have to live my own life, whether you allow me to or not. I'm grateful for all the times you were there to guide me when I needed you, but I'm not that little boy anymore. I don't know why you can't see that. God help me if I ever treat my own son this way."

"God help you see how bullheaded and stubborn you've become. And how foolish."

"I'm bullheaded? I'm stubborn?" Shawn let out a long, frustrated sigh.

"That's right. In my day, a man did what he was told, respected his father. Sacrificed if he had to. Gave up what he wanted for what was right."

"And did you like that arrangement?"

"It's not a question of did I like it. It's a question of duty and respect. Things you know little of."

"As I recall, all I ever heard is you complaining about how miserable you had it growing up with Grandpop. Is that how it works in this family? You have a miserable childhood, a tyrannical father whom you despise, stay under his control until you're liberated by his death, then it's your duty to pass the same thing on to your children? If that's the Collins legacy, it dies here with me. I will never treat my son that way."

"Why, you ungrateful little—" Collins shouted, rising to his feet. "How dare you talk to me in my house that way. How dare you talk about your grandfather that way. Get out." His whole arm pointed toward the front door.

"Is that really what you want?"

"It's what I demand," Collins said, still shouting. "Unless you're prepared to take back everything you've just said."

"How can I, Dad? I can say I'm not trying to hurt you. I can say I'm not doing these things out of spite. But if you can't let me start making my own choices without trying to manipulate me with guilt, we're not going to have much of a future."

"Then so be it," said Collins. He walked to the door and yanked it open. Shawn followed a few steps behind. "That woman has bewitched you, Shawn. She's taken you away from us—"

"Bewitched me?" Shawn stood right over him. "Elizabeth is the best thing that's ever happened to me. And she's not taken me away—you're the one putting me out. If you'd stop trying to run my life, we could get along fine. I came over here trying to share some things I've learned about the Christian faith, things I never understood before. I'm not telling you how to live your life. When you told me you didn't want to hear any more, what did I do? I backed off. Does that mean I don't feel strongly about my views? I've never felt more strongly about anything in my life, but I backed off. You know why? I was showing you respect. And that's all I'm asking from you in return. Just a little respect."

"What do you mean, telling me what you learned about the Christian faith?" Collins was still yelling even though Shawn's face was but inches from his own. "So *you're* a Christian now, is that it? And what does that make your mother and me?"

"Dad, did you hear a thing I said?"

"So now you're saying we're not Christians? I can't believe—"

"Dad, stop. It's not what I meant. There's a difference, that's all, between what I grew up learning and what I know now."

"I'll say there's a difference. You grew up learning respect, and now all you know about is being selfish and willful." Collins held the door open wider and stood out of Shawn's way.

"So that's it, then."

Collins motioned with his head for Shawn to leave.

Standing in the vestibule, Shawn turned and said, "Don't

expect me to come back here begging to get in your good graces. It's not going to happen."

Collins slammed the door shut, rattling the glass panes.

He and Shawn hadn't spoken two words since that moment, and that had suited Collins just fine. Ida had given him some trouble at first, but she was a good woman, knew her place in such matters.

The only other contact was a brief phone call to Ida when Shawn's wife got pregnant. But Collins stood his ground. The baby changed nothing. Three years later, Ida took ill. When the doctor confirmed their worst fears, Collins reluctantly agreed to allow Shawn to visit his mother as long as he gave fair warning before coming so Collins could exit the hospital first.

On her deathbed, Ida had made him promise he would reconcile with Shawn and Elizabeth. The power of the moment had been too strong to resist. Collins agreed, taking some comfort that he had never said anything about how or when. There had been no contact in the four years that followed.

Not until the boy had arrived the other day.

"Ian, does that upset you?" The words barely penetrated, more like raindrops on a tin roof. "Ian? Ian, are you listening?"

Collins finally focused on the mouth, then the face of Father O'Malley. Fear suddenly gripped him. If he didn't act fast, the father would be tempted to repeat the lecture Collins had just been spared. "No, no. I hear you."

"But did I upset you?"

"No, of course not. Why?"

"Your face has been growing steadily more sour the more I go on."

"It's just my breakfast turning over, Father. I'm fine. That's all very interesting, what you were saying. But you know, I probably ought to go check on the boy, and I'm sure you've got a busy day ahead of you." He stood up, hoping to strengthen the hint.

It worked. Father O'Malley stood with him and began walking toward the door. Collins quickly stepped ahead and lifted his black overcoat from the hook. "Thank you for the coffee, Ian. A treat to have real sugar for a change." He turned, allowing Collins to help him on with his coat.

"Now, Ian. You think hard about what I said in our little talk. The boy's been through a terrible ordeal. He needs normalcy and routine right now. I know you can't change all your ways in a matter of days, or replace a mother's love, but I'm just asking you . . . see what you can do to lighten his load. Would you do that for me, now? When Shawn gets home, maybe we can all sit down and figure something out together."

What an agonizing thought; Collins couldn't even allow an image of it to form in his head. "I'll let you know, Father." He opened the front door.

"I'll be off then, Ian. The Lord bless you and keep you. My, what a frosty morn."

Collins quickly closed the door. As he walked the cups and saucers back to the kitchen, he tried to ward off any sense of guilt about whether he had just lied to a priest. It wasn't lying in the true sense of the word, he decided. It was pretending to pay attention. And the fact that he didn't tell the father about the feud between him and Shawn wasn't a lie, either. Not telling someone a thing is not the same as telling them something that is untrue.

What's a few more weeks in purgatory? he thought. A small price to pay, considering. After rinsing the cups, he decided he better go check on the boy. He'd had plenty of time to do what he'd been told.

Collins dried his hands and braced himself for a fresh onslaught of Christmas cheer.

Nine

Patrick had set the wooden soldier aside as he worked his way through the box of decorations. He positioned it under the window so he could see it plainly at all times. By contrast the luster of the Christmas box had already faded. In about twenty minutes, he gathered a sufficient pile of decorations, made sure he could replace them in their assigned locations, then walked over to the wooden soldier and picked it up.

He couldn't just leave him here now that he'd discovered him. His grandfather would never allow him back up here to play. As he sat on an old cane chair, he stroked the soldier's helmet and thought through a plan. He remembered his friend Billy saying people only put things in attics they don't care about anymore. But they do care a little, otherwise they'd have thrown them out. This soldier must have been lying here for years, totally forgotten. It was caked in dust, like everything else up here. Maybe it was like Billy said, almost ready for the trash but not quite. Maybe his grandfather would let Patrick borrow it. He would promise not to hurt it. He wouldn't even play with it, just set it on his dresser next to the picture of his parents.

Then maybe if he was really good, his grandfather would

let him take it home when his father came to pick him up. Patrick smiled at that thought; his father would love this soldier.

He got up and carefully weaved his way back toward the stairs, cradling the soldier in his right arm. He'd come back for the decorations later. Barely halfway down the stairs, he heard footsteps coming up from the ground floor. He froze. *Quick,* he thought, *back up the stairs and put the soldier back, right where you found it. No, don't do that. Stick to the plan; it's a good plan. It might work. This soldier wouldn't give up and run away.*

Patrick took two more steps forward. The door opened. "Oh, hi. I was just coming down to—"

"Well, Father O'Malley is finally gone. Hey, what is that you've got there?"

"This? I found it up there, over by the—"

"Who said you could touch that?"

"Well, no one. I—"

"Give me that."

His grandfather lunged toward him. Patrick fell back on the stairs. His grandfather snatched the wooden soldier from Patrick and stormed past him back up the stairs.

"I'm sorry, sir. I wasn't taking it. I was just coming down to ask your permission."

"Don't ever touch this again. You hear me?"

He was already in the attic, his voice trailing off. Patrick wanted to run down the stairs and straight out the front door and never look back.

"Can't leave you alone for one hour," he heard his grandfather say, followed by what sounded like two swear words. "No respect at all. Guess I know where you got that from."

What should he do? Patrick hated this place. Why had Miss Townsend brought him here? Couldn't anyone else take care of him until they found his father? He'd rather live in an orphanage than here. He ran down the stairs, then across the hallway to his room. Once inside, he closed the door and jumped on the bed, bursting into tears, but cried into the pillow as quietly as he could.

⁂

He didn't know how long he had cried, but Patrick reached a point where he knew he was done. He felt a strange comforting feeling come over him just then. He sat up and looked into his mother's smiling face in the picture. In his mind he could hear her talking to him again, strong and clear. "It's okay, Patrick. You're not alone."

Patrick wanted to argue the point, but he didn't want the feeling of her nearness to leave. "But I feel like I am alone," he whispered. "You're in heaven; Daddy's at the war. And this man hates me, and I don't even know why. Nothing I do is right." He started breathing heavily, like he was about to cry again.

Through his mother's eyes a thought seemed to surface. She wasn't speaking it, but it was almost as strong. He remembered a bedtime story she'd read him one night during a terrible thunderstorm, about a time when the disciples were out on a boat. The wind had started to howl, and the waves began tossing the boat every which way. A storm much worse than this one, she had said. They had all began to fear the boat would capsize, and they would all drown.

The most amazing thing was that Jesus was sound asleep in the back of the boat. "Can you imagine that," his mother had said. "Being sound asleep when everyone else was afraid for their lives?"

Patrick remembered the disciples had woken Jesus up, saying something like, "Lord, don't you care if we die?" His mother had said sometimes we feel like we're all alone when we're afraid or in danger, but really we're not, not if the Lord is with us. Jesus woke up, walked to the edge of the boat, and ordered the wind and the seas to be calm and still. Instantly, they obeyed.

His mother had finished the story by saying that Jesus could sleep easily, even during a scary time like that, because he knew his heavenly Father had everything under control, and that he had authority even over things as powerful as the wind and the sea.

Patrick felt that same calm come over him just now. His grandfather was scary all right, but he wasn't more powerful than the wind and the sea. When Patrick's mind drifted back to the present, he was still staring at his mother's beautiful face. Then he heard the doorbell ring downstairs.

⌘

Collins didn't hear the doorbell ring the first time. It was normally loud enough to reach the rafters but not louder than his thoughts. This attic had always proved to be a place of conflicting emotions for him. Everywhere he turned he collided with memories, mostly painful ones.

Everything having to do with Ida just reminded him of how lonely he'd become since her passing. Everything to do with Shawn reminded him of either the pain of the last seven years or of the good times they had before the rift, times they could never have again.

Collins held the wooden soldier in the light and remembered the day it began as a block of wood from a pile behind the garage. It had been an overcast day late in the fall, before Shawn had ever met that woman he married. He had just headed back to college after yet another difficult visit back home. Collins decided to carve the soldier for Shawn as a peace offering. Shawn's room was filled with things Collins had carved for him throughout his childhood. He knew Shawn had recently developed an interest in World War I, so Collins modeled the soldier after Alvin York, a famous World War I hero.

As it turned out, his peace offering brought no peace between them.

At first, when Shawn came home, it seemed to work its magic once more. But by the end of the weekend, they were in conflict again and Shawn left in a huff. He stopped coming home on weekends after that.

The doorbell rang again.

Collins sighed as he set the soldier back in its assigned spot. "I'm coming," he yelled. *What now?* he thought. Before the boy came, he might enjoy a week to ten days without hearing that stupid bell. Now it rang twice in the same morning.

He made his way down the two flights of stairs and peeked out the curtains. A delivery truck of some kind, he thought. Now what's this all about? He put on his coat and opened the door. The cold hit him like a slap in the face. "What do you want?" he yelled through the vestibule door. A middle-aged man, bundled like a dog sled driver, stood there next to a large box.

"You Ian Collins?"

"Yes."

"This is for you, then."

"I haven't ordered anything."

The man looked down at his papers. "Says here it comes from Clark Street. From the landlord of an apartment building."

"I don't know anyone on Clark Street."

"Look, sir, you're Ian Collins, right? So I ain't at the wrong house. C'mon, it's freezing out here."

"I gotta pay for this?"

"No. The note says here it contains the belongings of one Elizabeth Collins, deceased. You even got the same last name. Guess the landlord had to rent the apartment out, needed to clear out her things."

"Well, I don't want it, why bring it here?"

The man looked down at his papers again. "It was authorized by someone named Townsend from Child Services. Look, do you mind? My nose is about to fall off out here. You don't want this, I can find someplace to dump it, but you still gotta sign for it."

"No, I better take it. Come in." He opened the outer door, then backed into the living room and out of the way. The man hauled it in on a wheel cart, dripping wet clumps of ice and snow all over the throw rug. "Right there will be fine," Collins said.

"Sign here, please."

Collins signed the form. The man stood there for a minute, apparently expecting a tip. "You think I'm going to tip you for something I never asked for?" Collins walked over toward the front door. The man shook his head in disgust and went out the way he came.

Collins closed the door. "What am I going to do with this?" he moaned. He heard a noise on the stair, looked up and saw the boy's face peeking out from behind the stair rails.

"What have you got me into now?" he said, surprising the boy.

Patrick ran back up the stairs. Collins heard his bedroom door close. He walked over and tried lifting the box, but it was too heavy. Maybe he should have just let the man throw it out like he said.

He was sure it was nothing but a boxful of trouble.

Ten

Captain Shawn Collins had flown seventeen bombing missions so far, but he'd never been this terrified before.

The 91st Bomb Group had already lost six planes to Nazi fighters on the way in to the target: a munitions factory in Bremen, Germany. Then as quickly as they came, the fighters disappeared. But then came a more terrifying adversary, for which the bombers had no defenses. Dozens of German antiaircraft gunners shot thousands of exploding canisters into the air disguised as harmless puffs of black smoke, each one unleashing jagged shards of molten metal in every direction. The boys nicknamed it "flak."

A direct hit from a single flak gun could instantly turn a bomber into a fireball of flaming debris. An indirect hit could knock out engines or flight controls, kill or maim anyone caught in the shrapnel's path.

Shawn, piloting a B-17 Flying Fortress nicknamed "Mama's Kitchen," tried to sound calm as he took in a damage report over the interphone from Nick Manzini, their starboard waist gunner.

"Hastings bought it, sir," Manzini said. "Took a big piece of metal in the neck. It ain't pretty. Looks like he went quick, though. Anderson is alive. Took some metal in the leg. Got a tourniquet around it. The bleeding has slowed a little, but he's in a state of shock. I can't even get him to talk to me."

Shawn forced his emotions to stay intact. The entire crew looked to him for stability. But these men were more than just gunners under his command; they'd trained together for months, had flown every mission together, so far without a single mishap.

"And Captain," Manzini continued, "that last flak burst open a brand-new window back here. Can't take too many more hits like that."

"Your guns operational?" Shawn asked.

"Let me check."

Shawn heard the sound of both machine guns being test fired.

"They're fine."

"Okay, get back to your station. You're gonna have to man both guns on the way home. Once out of Bremen, the fighters will hit us again. Make sure Anderson gets covered up, stays warm. Maybe he'll snap out of it in awhile and give you some help."

"Got it," said Manzini.

For several minutes, no one said a word. Only the droning engines and muffled explosions of flak bursts could be heard over their pounding hearts. The plane jumped and shuddered with each one. The crew didn't even react when another bomber just ahead fell out of formation and spun out of control, its left wing half shot off. No chutes were seen before it dropped out of sight.

Shawn tried to keep the plane steady, trying to keep his mind off the possibilities. With each new flak burst, he fought the temptation to steer the plane out of its path. The fact was, there were no safe paths; no amount of evasive action mattered. Survival seemed entirely a matter of fate or chance. Some, like Shawn, believed it a matter of Providence and prayed every prayer they knew. Others superstitiously clung to their rabbits' feet, lucky coins, saints' medals, or some other homemade talisman.

Every few moments, Shawn looked down at a photo of Patrick and Elizabeth. She'd sent it two months ago. Patrick was holding the baseball Shawn had caught at a Phillies game two seasons ago. Elizabeth . . . he still found it hard to believe he'd won the heart of such a beautiful woman. She could have been a cover girl from a fashion magazine, with her shoulder-length blonde hair, all natural, lightly curled, parted slightly to the right. Her lips were plump and soft, almost set in a pout, immanently kissable. The hardest part being married to her had been holding back the urge to deck guys who couldn't keep their eyes to themselves.

He thought about the first time they'd met. For him, it was love at first sight. For her, love came later. Her faith made her cautious. But that was okay. He had it bad enough for the both of them. She was sitting all alone at a table in the Penn State library. He couldn't take his eyes off her. His stares had finally gotten her attention. At first, she turned away, pretending she hadn't noticed. Then came that first smile. It happened on her third look up. He could still remember how it made him feel.

"It's time, Captain," said MacReady, the copilot.

"What?"

"Gotta turn the ship over to Davis."

"Oh, right," Shawn said. He reached down and flipped on the autopilot. "Okay, Nick. You've got the plane from here on. Make it count."

"Roger, Captain." The flak stayed heavy for ten more minutes. Every so often he heard a bang or a ping, as a stray piece of metal smacked into the fuselage. The plane seemed to be straining on the left side. Shawn feared one of the engines might have swallowed some shrapnel. Still, they held their place in the formation. He heard the bomb bay doors open.

Nick Davis simply announced "Bombs away" and closed the doors.

"How'd it look, Nick?" Shawn asked.

"A little hazy down there, but I think we nailed 'em."

Shawn braced himself. Once they cleared Bremen, the fighters would return.

The crawling speed of the bombers had always been a source of frustration for Shawn. On every mission he'd watch the enemy fighters dart in and around them at will, picking them off one at a time. And every time a bomber fell from the sky, ten men went down with it. Some to their deaths, the lucky ones to prison.

Shawn looked down at Elizabeth's picture again. "God, just let me get out of this alive." His thoughts were interrupted by Manzini yelling, "Here they come!" into the interphone.

The fighters.

Man, they were coming in fast. Shawn heard a loud explosion, followed by piercing screams.

A moment later, it felt like he was losing control of the plane.

Eleven

Patrick decided that this had officially become the second worst day of his life. It began being terrorized by his grandfather about the wooden soldier, then digressed into total, absolute boredom. After the scolding, Patrick hid in his room until lunch. He didn't plan on coming down, but his grandfather yelled "lunchtime" from the stairway like a troll growling from under the bridge.

It wasn't a suggestion.

Over peanut butter and jelly sandwiches and milk, they sat together in silence.

After lunch he politely excused himself and headed back to his room again. Just before going upstairs, he noticed the large brown box at the foot of the stairs. What could be inside, he wondered? Maybe his father had sent him something from England. Maybe Christmas presents. He looked back and saw his grandfather staring at him from the dining room table. He couldn't read the look so he made his way up the stairs, straight to his room.

He stayed there until dinner, playing with his toys on the bed, but didn't really have any fun. Dinner had gone much the same as lunch. After picking through a plate of dry meat loaf, corn, and potatoes, Patrick went back upstairs all alone. During the next two hours, he heard some of his favorite shows playing downstairs on the radio but couldn't work up enough nerve to go down.

He decided his grandfather must still be sore at him for touching the wooden soldier. Why else had he ignored Patrick so completely? As he lay back on his pillow, he wasn't sure what had hurt the most: getting yelled at, being alone for another day, missing his mom and dad, or the thought of never being able to play with the wooden soldier again.

This had been a day entirely devoid of childhood joys.

He glanced at his parents' photograph, first at his father's face then his mom's, finally focusing on her eyes. He hadn't been able to hear either of their voices since this morning. He imagined what she'd be telling him if she were here now. She'd say to get ready for bed, the right way. No shortcuts. Put all his toys away, change into his pajamas, wash his face, and brush his teeth. So that's what he did.

He could hear his grandfather making little noises downstairs. The smell of his cigar drifted up into the hallway. Patrick didn't recognize the radio show playing now, but whatever it was, every few seconds it made his grandfather laugh out loud. Once he laughed so hard it made Patrick laugh too. But he didn't want to laugh. He walked back to his bedroom, sighing as he closed the door. Would they ever laugh together? Would he ever see his grandfather even smile at him?

He folded the covers down and sat on the edge of his bed. He hadn't planned to look at his mother's picture anymore tonight. He was simply going to get on his knees and pray one of the shorter bedtime prayers she had taught him. But it was almost as if she was calling to him.

"I hate it here," he said. "It's only been one day, but it feels like a hundred. How many more days until Daddy gets here?"

He realized he was raising his voice. He buried his face in his hands. "Why did you leave me?" he said. "I can't do this all by myself. I'm just a boy."

As he poured out his sorrows, all the painful moments of the day floated through his mind one by one. Each received its own parcel of tears. When the parade of images ended, he felt a strange sensation, as if a peaceful presence had entered the room. He lifted his face, expecting to find someone there. He was still alone. But the peace was there. And it was strong. Somehow it washed away all his sadness and anger.

He glanced at his mother once more as he lay back on the bed; her smile seemed fresh and alive. He didn't even notice the light was still on. As he closed his eyes, it felt as if the bed rocked back and forth, almost like a cradle. He heard himself singing just before he drifted off to sleep, almost in a whisper: "Little ones to him belong; they are weak, but he is strong."

⁓

Three more inches of fresh snow had fallen during the night. In the predawn hours, Collins manned his post on the porch, coffee mug in hand, as the procession of defense plant workers marched down the street. Watching the falling snowflakes made him mad enough to spit. His was still the only house on the block with an unshoveled walk. That miserable Matthews boy five doors down said he would shovel it two days ago. Well, if he didn't come first thing after sunup, Collins would grab the first person he saw and pay them double.

He walked back into the house, hung up his coat, and stood over the box that had been delivered the day before. He'd been fighting his curiosity ever since the box arrived. He knew it was none of his business what was inside. His son should be getting back from England soon. By rights, he should just leave it alone and give it to Shawn as it sits.

He walked back into the kitchen and refilled his cup. As he sat at the dining room table, his eyes locked onto the box again. This was getting ridiculous. He should just go on over there and get it over with. The way it was sealed wouldn't be spoiled by him opening it. The four side flaps had just been folded in on themselves. He could put it back the way he found it, and no one would be the wiser.

He got up and walked to the stairs, leaning his ear upward to catch any movement from the boy. He waited a full minute, but there wasn't a sound. He walked to his favorite armchair, a brown stuffed affair contoured by thousands of hours spent in its folds. He slid the matching ottoman over with his foot and sat on it. He listened again for the boy. Quietly, he wrestled the top flaps free of their hold and peered inside.

He didn't know what he'd expected, but this was a disappointment. Just a box of clothes folded sloppily, an assortment of pots and pans and cheap silverware, some framed pictures stacked sideways like a deck of cards. Then down there at the bottom was a cardboard shoe box tied around with string. He hoped to find something to warrant the level of distraction this thing had caused him over the last twenty-four hours.

After staring a few minutes, he was struck by a thought that made him both sad and angry. This box represented all his son had acquired in this world. He and his wife were just renting that apartment on Clark Street, furniture too. He probably couldn't get five bucks for the stuff inside this box at a church rummage sale. So, for the contents of this box, Shawn had turned down an opportunity to run a healthy, growing business, which had more than quadrupled in size since the start of the war. A business that would have been entirely his at this point. And because the business manufactured defense materials, Shawn would have likely received a deferment from the military to keep it running. He would be home and a rich man right now. Instead, Shawn was risking his neck every day over Germany, sending home just enough money each month to sustain what Collins was now looking at in this box.

What a waste, thought Collins. What a total waste.

He was about to close the box back up when the little shoe box caught his attention. Perhaps at least it contained something of value. He wiggled the string loose without untying it and lifted the lid. Just a boxful of folded papers. A bunch more of nothing. They appeared to be letters, at least on top. He thumbed through the stack, half hoping to find at least some stock or bond certificates. But they were all just letters, must be fifty of them. He laid them back in the box and was just about to close the lid when he saw the words "with all my love, Shawn" at the bottom edge of the first one.

He stared at it for the longest time, then set them all down carefully. He noticed something small sliding from the corner of the shoe box, tied together with a piece of brown twine. A pair of rings. A wedding band and another ring with the tiniest diamond setting he'd ever seen. They would have belonged to Shawn's wife. Just stuck there in the box like that.

Somewhere deep inside, a flame of sympathy flickered to life. These were all letters from Shawn to his wife and the rings he had placed on her finger at a wedding Collins had refused to attend. A wife Collins had never allowed himself to get to know but whom his son loved with all his heart. He recognized Shawn's handwriting. His wife had even saved all the envelopes. A knot formed in Collins's throat. He hated how it felt and wished he could will it away.

The knot was the realization that he and Shawn did have

something in common now after all these years. The love of a wife and the terrible anguish that follows when you realize she is gone. By now, Shawn had to have been told. Collins missed his Ida so bad just then, almost as badly as the moment her eyes had closed for the last time. Sometimes it seemed like it happened just yesterday. Sometimes like it was a hundred years ago. And sometimes—and this was the most peculiar feeling—it felt like it had never happened, like he had made the whole relationship up in his head, like he had always been just an old man living alone.

He realized where all this brooding was taking him and did not wish to go there. It was a dark empty place without a stitch of comfort, a refuge for the weak and sentimental. And Collins was neither of those. He swallowed hard, quickly dropping the letters back in place. He closed the lid to the shoe box and looped the string back around it. He set the shoe box back in its proper corner and snapped the top flaps shut.

He was startled by a noise on the stairway. "Grandfather?" a young voice called out.

Collins moved away from the box and looked up. It was Shawn coming down the stairs in his pajamas, wiping the sleep out of his eyes. "Shawn," Collins said, a tenderness in his voice that hadn't been there in years. "It's too early for you to be up, son. A growing boy needs his sleep."

"Huh?" the boy said, rubbing his eyes.

Collins started to walk up the stairs, extending his arms to the boy. But something was wrong. He couldn't catch it at first. Then he realized. The hair was too light, and the face was off somehow. "Oh no," he said, suddenly aware of his mistake.

It wasn't Shawn. How could he have been so foolish?

Twelve

Patrick awakened with the same peaceful sensation he had at bedtime. The sun shone brightly through the blinds. His bed felt soft and warm beneath the blankets. A vague memory of a pleasant dream was slipping from his mind, involving his grandfather of all things. Only a snippet remained, but in the dream his grandfather had met him halfway down the stairs and even talked kindly to him. If Patrick had it right, he'd even tucked him back into bed. It didn't make any sense, but it was a pleasant way to start the day.

He sat up, pulled off his covers, and smiled at the picture of his parents, this time focusing on his father's face. Soon he'll be home, Patrick thought. Miss Townsend had promised. Maybe his grandfather would let him call her today and find out when.

He got out of bed, stretched and yawned, then turned to make the bed. As he did, he remembered the wooden soldier in the attic. There had to be a way to see him again. He wouldn't break it. How could he make his grandfather see? Other kids his age broke things, but Patrick wasn't like that. His neighbor, Mrs. Howard, said he was the only little boy she had ever trusted in her parlor.

He straightened the rest of his room, changed his clothes, and went into the bathroom. Along the way, he stopped and eyed the attic door. *He's up there all by himself*, Patrick thought. In his mind, the soldier was well on his way to becoming a living thing.

When he finished in the bathroom, he went downstairs. The living room was empty. He walked into the kitchen and peeked around the corner. The kitchen was empty too. He began to panic. He hadn't heard any noise upstairs. Was his grandfather still upstairs? It was starting to feel like the bad dream he had two nights ago. He was just about to run upstairs when he heard footsteps coming from below, behind a doorway in the dining room. His grandfather emerged from the basement, wiping his hands on his pants.

"So you're up," he said, closing the door. "I suppose you want something to eat."

Patrick breathed a sigh of relief.

"I've got some oatmeal made in a pot if you want it. Help yourself."

Patrick wanted to remind him he was only seven. Seven-year-olds weren't supposed to fix their own breakfasts. "Thank you," he said. "Is there any milk, sir?"

"Some in the icebox. Smell it first."

After eating breakfast by himself, he began to dread the day ahead. A half hour in his grandfather's presence and his morning joy had evaporated. He got up from the table and cleaned up his mess. As he worked, he tried building his nerve to just walk right into the living room and talk things out with his grandfather. First, he'd ask him about calling Miss Townsend. Then about what was in that cardboard box. Maybe even about the wooden soldier in the attic.

Well, maybe not about the wooden soldier just yet.

Patrick tiptoed in and stood in front of him, silent as a

sentry. He was reading the newspaper. Patrick hoped to catch him when he changed pages. The doorbell rang, startling them both. His grandfather jumped in his seat, newspaper pages flapping in the air. Patrick jumped back.

"What are you doing?" Collins asked Patrick, rising to his feet.

"I-I was just standing here. I—"

"Who is that now?" Collins muttered as he answered the door. "Oh, great," he said, standing on his tiptoes, looking out the front door window. "What does she want?"

"Who is it?" Patrick asked, hoping the answer was Miss Townsend.

Collins sighed as he put on his coat. "You better step back. I open this door and you're going to freeze."

Patrick backed halfway into the dining room.

"Hurry up, old man. I'm freezing out here." A muffled woman's voice yelled through the door. It couldn't be Miss Townsend, he thought. The woman had some kind of accent.

The door opened on a big black blob of a woman stomping the snow off her boots in the vestibule. She marched through the threshold like she was in her own home and handed Collins her black gloves. As she parted with a fur hat, Patrick noticed her black hair was tightly woven in a bun, thick gray streaks on the sides. She wore a hairnet that seemed to emanate from a dark hole in the center of her forehead. She was holding some kind of covered plate, which she set down on the coffee table. Collins closed the door behind her with a frown.

"Morning, Mrs. Fortini," Collins said. "What brings you over so early in the morning?" He didn't sound pleased.

"Is that him?" she said, handing Collins her coat and staring right at Patrick. Her smile, set against her jovial face, gave her the appearance of a happy pumpkin. She moved toward him, arms reaching out. Instinctively, he backed up farther into the dining room. Even beneath her coat, she was dressed in black, right down to her stockings. But her eyes were so bright and caring. In a moment, he was engulfed in her arms.

"What a beautiful boy. You must be so proud," she said, pulling back slightly. She bent down and grabbed his cheeks in her icy hands, squeezing them affectionately. He couldn't help but smile.

Collins walked over to the coffee table and peeked beneath the tinfoil cover. "Cookies," he said with disgust. "I see what's going on here. That Miss Townsend send you over here? Yesterday she sets Father O'Malley on me, and today she sends you. Well, I've had just about as much of that young woman as I'm gonna take."

"What are you going on about, you old stinker?"

"The boy!" he yelled back. "She thinks I can't take care of the boy."

Instantly, the woman put her hands, big as catchers' mitts, over Patrick's ears. But he could still hear most of what she said. She said she didn't have any idea what he was talking about, that she'd never heard of a Miss Townsend, and that he had some nerve talking so harshly in front of "the boy" after all he'd been through. His grandfather made some kind of reply, though he didn't quite catch it. But his expression was satisfying, like a child who'd just received a licking. She must be a powerful woman, Patrick thought. He instantly decided he liked her a great deal.

She took her palms off his ears and reached over toward the covered plate. She pulled out a thick chocolate chip cookie. "Do you like this kind?"

"Very much."

"Well, here," she said, handing it to him. "You go sit over at the table, and I'll fix you some milk. Can't have cookies without milk. You got any milk?" she asked Collins over her shoulder.

"I don't know. He used it last. Ask him."

"There's a little left," Patrick answered. "Maybe half a glass."

She moaned as she straightened up. "Well, I'll get that. You go have a seat." She turned to face Collins. "When's the last time the milkman came?"

"He was due this morning, but he didn't show. I don't normally run out."

"He probably refused to walk through your snowbanks. You know you're the only one on the block who doesn't have your walk cleared?"

"I'd hired the Matthews boy to do it a couple of days ago, but he hasn't shown up."

"You didn't hear? He had a birthday this week and joined the army."

"Would have been nice if he told me!"

"Well, you go back to your paper, and I'll get Patrick his milk. And you leave a note for that milkman about Patrick, so he can start dropping off an extra quart. Growing boys need their milk."

She headed for the kitchen. Collins just stood there under the arch between the living and dining rooms, a stunned look on his face. Patrick watched as she rummaged through the cabinets, then the icebox. "This is terrible," she said.

He looked back at his grandfather, who was still standing in the same spot. Collins shook his head and sighed. "What's the matter now?" he asked.

Mrs. Fortini stormed out of the kitchen. "You've got nothing here for a little boy."

"We're just fine."

"You're not fine. There's no treats, no snacks, no cereal, no—"

"He's been eating oatmeal in the morning."

"Is that what you're going to feed him every morning?"

"He's only going to be here till his father comes to get him. Few days at the most."

"He can't eat the same thing every morning. Maybe you can, but little boys need variety in their diet."

"He's fine, Mrs. Fortini." He looked at Patrick. "Aren't you." It wasn't a question.

"Don't ask him," she interrupted. "Do you honestly expect him to disagree with you? Here," she said, holding out her hand. "You've got money. Give me some, and I'll go down to Hodgins's and buy something decent."

Collins just stood there looking confused.

"Come on," she said.

"My wallet's upstairs."

"Not a big problem. I'll wait right here."

Patrick stood up and lifted his glass off the table.

She turned and said in a gentler tone, "What are you doing?"

"I'm just cleaning up."

"I'll do that. Would you like another cookie?"

"Yes, I would."

"Are you still here?" she said to Collins. He turned and walked toward the stairs. "And don't forget the ration books," she said as he climbed out of sight. "Both red and blue. I haven't got enough for both of us." She walked over and snatched another cookie from the tray. "You eat that," she said. "I'll clean up and write myself a little list."

A few minutes later, Collins came down with some cash and his ration books. Mrs. Fortini was just finishing her list at the table. She got up and inspected his cash offering, then her list. "That should be enough. Did this government lady give you any additional ration coupons for your grandson?"

"Uh, now that you mention it, no she did not."

"You know cash is never enough anymore. You don't have sufficient points, and you don't buy."

"I know."

"Well, I suggest you get right on that phone and ask them to send some over. I'll use some of mine for now, but I'll need them replaced. By rights, he has them coming."

"All right, I'll take care of it."

"Patrick, would you like to go with me?" She walked over and put on her coat, stuffing the cash and ration books in the oversized pockets.

"He can't go out there. It's freezing."

"It's not as bad as yesterday," she said. "The sun is shining. It's stopped snowing. The wind isn't even blowing. You have a winter coat, right, Patrick?"

"And a hat and gloves," he said.

"See?"

"He'll catch a cold, and then that Miss Townsend will be breathing fire out her nose."

"Mr. Collins, little boys play outside in the snow all the time, and they generally live to tell the tale."

Collins sighed again and rolled his eyes.

"Any more excuses?"

He turned and started into the living room.

"Where you going?"

"To get his coat and gloves," he said.

She bent down and whispered in Patrick's ear, "See, he didn't want you to get sick. He really does care about you. We just have to help him see."

Thirteen

Miss Katherine Townsend worked on the third floor of a bland office building in downtown Philadelphia, about five blocks west of Independence Hall. She sat in her tiny windowless cubicle as she did every morning, sipping lukewarm coffee, surrounded by a sea of tiny cubicles. All occupied by women. The window offices were reserved for the management positions, all occupied by men.

She didn't know how much longer she could put up with this job at Child Services. So many tragedies to wade through each day and only a handful of cases over the last two years where she felt she had made any difference at all. But she held in her hands a file containing the most hopeful case she'd had in a long time.

Little Patrick Collins.

Just thinking about Patrick again brought an involuntary smile to her face. But it was so hard to think of him stuck in that house with that terrible old man. All day yesterday she'd fought off the impulse to drive down to Allingdale and check on him. Her job protocols mandated she stay away the first few days unless there was proof the child was in some danger; give the principals in the case time to get used to each other.

She decided she couldn't wait any longer; forget the protocols, she would see Patrick today.

He might just be the most handsome little boy she had ever seen. Such bright blue eyes, and that dimpled smile. More than how delightful it looked on his face, the fact that it appeared at all was what so intrigued her. She'd seen so many children who'd endured far less hardship than Patrick completely lose their smiles; she'd wondered if they'd ever return. She had never seen a child react to so much adversity with so much composure and poise. Few adults could have handled the situation with as much character.

"Have lunch with me?"

Speaking of adults lacking character, she thought as she turned to face Bernie Krebb, her supervisor.

"I'm sorry, Mr. Krebb. I have other plans." Krebb had asked her out almost every day since she started this job. This was her standard response.

"Mr. Krebb, Mr. Krebb. It's Bernie, Kath. How many times are we going to have to go over this?"

She looked up at his yellow eyes and bulbous nose. A limp cigarette dangled from his lips, the smoke wafting upward, irritating his eyes. He always acted like he meant for it to do that. Of course, he was wearing his hat. Always the hat, even indoors. Trying to obscure his balding head.

"Well, first off, it's Miss Townsend, Mr. Krebb. Not Kath or Katherine. And I agree . . . how many times do we have to go over this?" She knew opposing him wouldn't help her career, but the fact was he made her skin crawl. He repulsed her in every way a man could be repulsive. He was even married with two kids. She vowed if he ever laid a hand on her, she'd do her best to break his nose.

He walked in and sat on her lone office chair. His expression shifted to slightly business, but he still kept what he obviously thought was his most alluring smile. "I thought it might be better we talk about this in more pleasant surroundings, say at Rosario's over a plate of linguini, but if you insist on being such a cold fish . . ."

"What are you talking about?"

He looked around as though he didn't want anyone to hear, then leaned forward. "Been talk upstairs about making cutbacks in this department."

"And . . . ?"

"C'mon, Kath. You know your numbers are down. And your monthly gas consumption is higher than any of the others."

Katherine looked down. They'd had this conversation before. Not about the cutbacks, but about how much time she took with each case, about getting too personally involved and emotionally attached. Most of the girls played it by the book, set the kids up as quickly as possible, then moved on to the next case. "So what are you saying?"

"I'm saying when the cutbacks come—"

"Now you're saying it's definite?"

"Just a matter of time. They turned down our request for gas increases for the new year. Since our expenses are still going up . . . well, you figure it out."

Katherine sighed. Even with its downsides, she didn't want to lose this job. The alternatives were waitressing or becoming Rosy the Riveter in some factory.

"I've been warning you—don't get so attached to these kids. You ain't paid to love 'em. The way I see it, unless a guy like me intervenes, the boys upstairs are going to go strictly by the numbers. Bad time of year to be stuck without a job."

"And what would it take to get you to intervene on my behalf?" she asked, as if she didn't know. Once he had told her how much she reminded him of Rita Hayworth, that she'd look just as beautiful with the right dress on. He loved the way her brown eyes lit up when she smiled. It almost sounded poetic, and she might have even enjoyed the compliment if it hadn't been spewing out from such a putrid stump like Bernie Krebb.

"For starters, stop turning me down for lunch," he said. "Then we can take it from there. You know, the way things are meant to go, one thing to another. I'm not such a bad guy, Kath. Ask around."

What an idiot, she thought. All the girls were as disgusted by him as she was. Some were just a little more ambitious or brought up a little differently. And she hadn't seen any of them move out of their cubicles. He had no clout in the agency. He was just a pathetic little man who thought way too highly of himself. "Mr. Krebb. It's not going to happen. Not in a thousand years, not in a thousand lifetimes. You're a married man, and I—"

"Don't let that bother you. My wife and I have an understanding."

"I'm sure you have. But it's more than that." How could she say what she was thinking? *You make me sick. To see you is to want to throw up.*

Just then the phone rang.

"I've got to take this," she said. "I'm expecting a call."

He stood up and stepped back into the threshold. "Think about what I said. I'd hate to lose you."

The phone rang again. She turned to answer it, giving Krebb as much shoulder and back as she could. "Hello? Child Services, Miss Townsend speaking." She could hear Krebb's footsteps as he walked away.

"Miss Townsend? Major Jennings, Army Air Force. We

spoke earlier. I have some information for you about Captain Collins."

"Is he on his way? Please tell me he's on his way."

"I'm afraid it's not that simple."

"I don't understand. How could they not let him go after what's happened."

"I didn't say they wouldn't let him go. You're getting ahead of me. All I've been able to verify is that the approval for his leave has been authorized. I can't tell you anything beyond that. My counterpart in England had to cut short our conversation. I could hear air raid sirens going off in the background. He said to call back in a few hours, but with the time difference, I don't think I'll get anything more until tomorrow."

"I appreciate your candor, Captain. And I really appreciate you calling me back. But please stay on it, if you don't mind. I've got a little boy here who really needs his daddy right now. I think I mentioned his mother died recently in a car accident."

"I understand, Miss Townsend. If I hear anything at all, I'll be sure to let you know." He paused for a moment, then said, "But you know how slow things move in the military."

"I understand. But please don't let this fall through the cracks."

"I'll do the best I can," he said.

Fourteen

It's a well-known fact that children and adults generally have differing opinions about the value of snow. To one, it conjures visions of downhill sledding; to the other a car sliding downhill. To one it's a snowman; to the other a snow shovel. But a white Christmas is different. On that, both young and old generally agree. If the weathermen were right, this could be just such a Christmas. All but the most hardened of souls enjoy a white Christmas.

One such hardened soul stood inside his vestibule, watching a grandson he hardly knew and a next-door neighbor he barely understood walking down the snowy sidewalk of his home on Chestnut Street in Allingdale, bundled up in winter attire. Allingdale was a little township just south of Philly. Mrs. Fortini said she was taking the boy to Hodgins's Grocery, down on Clifton Ave. But she was heading in the wrong direction. Hodgins's was east on Chestnut. She was heading west toward Bartram Ave. There was nothing in that direction except a Jewish cemetery.

He wondered what idiocy was running through her head.

∽

The late morning sun had already eroded the rough edges from the early morning snow, turning the mounds and snowbanks into soft, rounded curves. Some of the snow had formed into little ice puddles on the sidewalks. Mrs. Fortini shuffled her feet as they moved along, barely lifting them off the ground with each step.

"Why are you walking that way?" Patrick asked.

"How am I walking?" she asked.

"Like this." Patrick tried to imitate her shuffle.

Mrs. Fortini laughed. "Because I'm old, and because you're too little to drag my big body home."

"What?"

"My neighbor across the street slipped two days ago on the ice and broke her hip. It was terrible. She couldn't move and she was in so much pain. I didn't see her fall, but I looked out my window and saw a teenaged boy dragging her back to her house. I am much bigger than she is, and you are much smaller than that boy."

Patrick smiled. "I don't want you to fall."

"So it's okay I walk like this?" she said, exaggerating her shuffling steps.

"It's okay."

Just being outside in the fresh, cold air made Patrick happy. Being with Mrs. Fortini made him happy. She was the perfect age, had the perfect shape, and the perfect personality to be a grandmother, so he decided to pretend that's what she was. He was too young to remember Grandma Collins, and he had never met his mother's parents. His mom said they were already in heaven way before he was born. At least they were all together now, he thought. He looked down at Mrs. Fortini's huge gloved hand holding onto his, then back up at her pleasant face. Her eyes were squinting in the sun, but he could see she was smiling.

Today had to be a better day just by the way it started. "Which house is yours?" he asked.

They stopped and she turned around. "We walked past it a little while ago. See that one back there, right next to your grandfather's?"

"The one with the little white fence around it?"

"That's the one."

The house was similar to his grandfather's, except it had a porch instead of a vestibule, and it was painted green instead of gray. And it had Christmas decorations, like the rest of the neighborhood. Many had wreaths on their doors, snowmen in their yards; some even had their lampposts wrapped in red and green ribbon. A slight movement caught his eyes. He looked past Mrs. Fortini's porch and noticed his grandfather standing in his vestibule, staring in their direction. When their eyes met, he turned and walked back into the house.

"Have you lived there long?" Patrick asked.

"Since your father was a boy not much older than you."

"Really?"

"That's right. And he played with my two little boys. They used to make snowmen together in the front yard."

"I like snowmen."

"And they went sledding together and played ball together."

"My dad's a great baseball player."

"He certainly was."

Patrick didn't like the sound of that. "Not was . . . *is*."

"You're right . . . is. I just meant he doesn't get to play much now that he's grown up." She gave him a big smile, and they continued down the sidewalk.

As he walked along he noticed how different all the houses were here than around Clark Street. He was used to homes all connected together. No one had front yards or backyards. Just sidewalks and alleys. And he hardly ever saw trees except at the parks.

When they came to the corner, they turned left. This street was even more different. It only had houses on one side. All down the other side was a tall stone wall. Mrs. Fortini looked both ways then led them across the street and onto the sidewalk nearest the wall. He couldn't see over the top. "What's over there?" he asked.

"There? Do you really want to know?"

He nodded.

"It's a cemetery."

"Oh," he said quietly.

"Do you want to see?"

"Yeah, but how can I?"

"Come here." She lifted him up. "Hold on to the stones."

All along the top edge of the wall, different colored rocks stuck out at various angles. He peered over the top at a huge field of gravestones and monuments, as far as the eye could see. "Must be thousands of 'em," he said.

"At least."

"My mom is buried in one of these places. Well, her body is."

"You're right, Patrick. Just her body is. She's still alive, you know."

"I know," he said, a tinge of sadness now starting to surface. "But I wish she were alive with me."

"One day you'll be together again. You know that? And when that day comes, you'll never be apart."

He liked Mrs. Fortini more and more. "What are all those strange stars on the stones?"

"That's called the Star of David."

"Like David in David and Goliath?"

"The very same. This is a Jewish cemetery. They use the Star of David like a symbol, the way we use a crucifix."

"What's a crucifix?"

"You don't know? It's the cross where Jesus died."

"Oh, we just call ours a cross."

"That's right," she said. She paused a moment. "One of my boys is buried in another cemetery not far from our church."

"One of your boys died?"

"Yep. He was stationed at Pearl Harbor when the Japanese attacked. So I know just how you feel. Do you remember Pearl Harbor?"

"Sort of. I was five. That's what started the war, right? All those ships blowing up? I saw the newsreels a few times."

"That's right. My son was a sailor on one of those ships. But he's with Jesus now. You know, Patrick, death doesn't have to always be a sad thing, and cemeteries don't always have to be sad places."

Patrick didn't know what to say. They both seemed like pretty sad things to him, pretty much all the time.

"They are sad for a while, but we just have to remember a few things, and the sadness soon goes away."

"What things?"

"Well, your mama believed in Jesus, right?"

"Very much," he said. "So do I."

"So did my Frankie. One minute he was asleep on a boat, and the next minute he was in heaven. I believe that. By the time I heard the terrible news, he was already five days in heaven. I cried for a solid week. I couldn't sleep. I couldn't eat. I'd go to mass every day, but all I could do was think about Frankie and that I would never see him again. And then the crying would start all over again."

"That all sounds pretty sad to me. I thought dying wasn't supposed to be sad."

"You're right, I did say that. But I haven't told you the best part. One morning I was sitting in the pew, crying again, and the priest was talking. And then I heard the words of Jesus, like he was talking right to me. 'I am the resurrection and the life. He who believes in me, though he may die, yet shall he live. And whoever lives and believes in me shall never die.'"

"Jesus spoke to you?"

"In a way. It was the priest's voice. He was quoting from one of the Gospels in his homily. But it was as if the priest stopped talking and Jesus started talking. And I realized, my Frankie believed in Jesus. He prayed to him every day. He did as a little boy, and he told me he still did every day in all his letters from Hawaii."

"My mom believed in Jesus . . . with all her heart."

"So those words are the same for her . . . and for you. I realized that I would see my Frankie again. It would just be a long time. I remembered how much I cried when he left for the navy. But that time I wasn't crying because I would never see him again, but because he was taking a long trip, and I'd miss seeing his beautiful face and his big hugs. But I knew I would see him again. When I got the news about his ship being sunk, I cried because I was thinking I would never see Frankie again. But it wasn't true. It was just that God was taking him on a longer trip than we had planned. But we will meet again. And the next time we meet, we will never be apart."

"I will see my mom again," he said.

"Yes, you will. And it's okay to cry, because we always cry when people we love go on long trips. But it's a different kind of crying than for people who think they will never see each other again. Do you understand?"

Patrick nodded and smiled.

"Seen enough?" she asked.

"Uh-huh." She released her grip and he slid down the wall to the sidewalk.

They walked in silence for another two blocks until they came to a wide, busy street lined with all kinds of shops and stores. "Make sure you hold my hand as we cross," she said.

A trolley car hurried by, spraying wet snow several feet in the air as it passed. Patrick ducked behind Mrs. Fortini but could tell by her scream that she didn't escape. She turned around, her face angry, half-covered in brown slush. Her coat was covered with more of the same. "Look at me," she snapped.

Patrick started to laugh; he couldn't help it. "I'm sorry," he said.

His laughter caused her to laugh. She brushed herself off as best she could. "If it makes you happy," she said, "then I am happy."

Patrick didn't understand what she meant, but he was glad her smiling pumpkin face had returned. They hurried across the street, just in time to beat another soaking from a speeding car. "The sun is melting all the snow," he said.

"Not all," she said. "It's always like this on Clifton Ave. The cars and trolleys turn it into mush. Oh, look," she said sadly. "Look at that line." Her eyes focused on a butcher's shop, two stores up from Hodgins's Grocery. At least thirty women of varying ages, purses tucked tightly under their overcoats, poured out of the store in single file. They huddled close to the buildings, trying to avoid being baptized in slush as cars sped by. An elderly man, who wore a wrinkled coat covering white overalls, stood by the front door, admitting four or five women at a time, after about the same number left the store.

"I need to pick up some meat while we're out," Mrs. Fortini said. "I'm going to have to get in line now or we'll be here all day. You think if I gave you my list, you could go into the grocery store by yourself and pick out some things?"

"Me?"

"I think you could do it. But you don't have to if you don't want."

"What if I can't find something? What if I don't know some of the words on your list?" Patrick had only just begun to learn how to read, although both his mom and his teacher had said he read as good as some kids in the fourth grade.

"Mr. Hodgins is a very nice man. You tell him you're Mr. Collins's grandson, and he'll treat you especially nice. Just get everything you can, then ask him to tell you any words you can't understand."

"What if it gets too heavy for me to carry?"

"Then just set it on the counter and come get me. Mr. Hodgins won't mind."

"All right, if you think I can."

"I know you can. You are a very bright boy."

Fifteen

On her way to visit Patrick, Katherine drove the last several blocks behind a Western Union truck. She had no family of her own, so it carried no dark forebodings, but she noticed how it drew the eye of every passerby like a magnet. As it turned onto Clifton Avenue, three older mothers carrying their shopping bags stopped dead in their tracks and stared. Katherine saw dread on each face. When it turned left onto Bartram Avenue, a teenaged boy riding a bike stopped so fast he almost went over the handlebars. *Probably has an older brother in the war*, she thought. It was as if the Grim Reaper himself had shed his black robe and sickle for a brown uniform and telegram.

Katherine had visited several families just after they'd received the telegram bearing the most dreaded words of all:

```
The Secretary of War desires to express his
    deep regret that your son was killed in
    action in defense of his country . . .
```

When the truck got to Collins's street, fortunately it turned in the opposite direction. *Now there's a job even worse than mine*, she thought. She pulled up to the curb next to Collins's house and instantly felt herself getting tense. *He's just an old man*, she thought. *He doesn't bite. Do it for Patrick.*

She knocked hard on the glass vestibule door then buried her hands in her coat pockets. She was about to knock again when the front door finally opened. "Afternoon, Mr. Collins."

He stood there glaring at her, a lit cigar sticking out of his face. He wore a wrinkled coat over a thin white T-shirt, pajama bottoms, and slippers.

"The boy's not here."

"Ah, the boy. What was his name again? Let me look at my paperwork."

"What do you want?"

"I'm just checking up, seeing how Patrick's doing. It is part of my job, you know."

"He's doing fine." He started closing the door.

"Excuse me, Mr. Collins. Do you mind? I've driven out all this way from downtown."

"Good for you." He turned and stepped back into the threshold.

"You are so rude. Anyone ever tell you that?"

"I'm not rude, I'm old. Anyone ever tell you what happens when you get old?"

Katherine smiled. She didn't want to, but it was a good line. Mr. Collins smiled also. It was an awkward moment for them both.

He stepped into the vestibule but still didn't offer to let her inside. "He just went for a walk with my next-door neighbor, Mrs. Fortini. She's running an errand for me down the road on Clifton Avenue, buying some things for the boy—I mean my grandson. Which way you come?"

"Down Baltimore Pike, then MacDade Boulevard."

"Then you rode right past Clifton Avenue to get here. It's

that wide road the trolleys run on. That's where they are. Check Hodgins's Grocery or Ray's Meats. Two best bets."

"Do you know when they'll be back?"

"You got a woman shopping with money in her hand. Anybody's guess. But you should have no trouble finding them. Just turn back the way you came. Park on the first main road you come to. Look for a big Italian woman all dressed in black dragging around a little Irish boy."

Katherine looked at her watch. She had only given herself fifteen minutes for the visit, unless she had found Patrick in a bad state. She could waste all that and more hunting through crowded shops looking for them.

"Heard anything more on the boy's father, when he might be back?"

First, it's the boy, she thought. *Now the boy's father . . . though talking about his own son.* "Not yet," she said. "Talked to an officer this morning who's looking into it."

"What are they saying?"

"I haven't been able to find out anything other than the approval for his leave has gone through."

"Shouldn't be long, then. In the First War it took weeks crossing the Atlantic by boat. Now with these planes, he should probably be in here in a couple of days, don't you think?"

"I don't know, Mr. Collins. I'll let you know if I hear anything more. I really have to go if I'm going to catch Patrick before I head back."

He walked back into the house and started to close the door. "Oh, I almost forgot," he said, turning around. "I'll need some ration coupons for the boy. Mrs. Fortini is using hers and mine to buy some supplies."

"That's right. I meant to give them to you the other night." She dug them out from her satchel and gave them to him. "Sorry about that."

He stood in the doorway for a moment, looking at them through the glass, as if trying to figure a way for them to penetrate the glass without letting her in.

"I suppose you'll have to open the door, after all."

He did, just a crack, and she slid them through. "Just trying to keep out the cold," he said. "If you miss him on Clifton, I'll tell him you stopped by." He walked back into the house and closed the door.

"Do that," she said to the closed door, watching her breath vaporize then disappear on the glass.

One more group of four ladies, then it would be her turn to get into Ray's Meats. Seeing the others made Mrs. Fortini realize she'd forgotten to pick up her jar of waste fat back at the house. The other ladies had theirs in hand. She'd been growing her jar all week, straining every last ounce of cooking oil, bacon grease, and used-up lard she could find. With the new rations it would have netted her at least three or four red points, which she could have used to buy more meat.

Collins had given her plenty of cash, but since the war, cash wasn't enough anymore. The Office of Price Administration, or OPA, kept strict controls on the prices and quantities of any food sold in stores. At first, she thought she'd never get it down; the whole system seemed far too complicated. Now it was just part of life. Red stamps for meat, fish, poultry, and the like; blue stamps for everything else. When it came to meat, each cut was given a different set of points. Ground round could be four points per pound, pork chops five points, a brisket seven.

As an incentive, the OPA rewarded people extra points for collecting certain things. Oddly enough, waste fat was among them. She smiled looking at the row of ladies in front of her, dutifully cradling their big jars of fat like grandbabies. Hard to imagine fat ever being a good thing. But they said fat contained something they could recycle into material for making explosives and different kinds of medicines. She couldn't imagine how that was possible.

All she knew was, you turn in your jar of fat, you get more meat.

Once inside, she became part of another line that wrapped in a horseshoe past the glass case. There wasn't as much chatter in the store as usual. A moment later, she understood why. Standing next to the scale, as out of place as a pig in a parlor, was a man in a black suit and tie. Everyone knew he was an OPA man, probably making his rounds of all the butcher shops in the area: checking the scales, keeping the merchants honest, making everyone nervous. She used her time in line to eye the case and add up her points, see what combination of meat and ration stamps she could put together.

She wondered how Patrick was making out at Hodgins's Grocery. He was such a beautiful little boy. Somehow she had to make that old buzzard see. She had promised her best friend, Ida, before she had died, that she would do whatever she could to get father and son back together again. It had become a topic in her morning prayers every day since Ida had passed.

She didn't know how, but she had a growing impression that, somehow, Patrick was the key.

Sixteen

Patrick entered Hodgins's Grocery like a brave explorer through some uncharted jungle. He had never been inside a store without holding his mother's hand. Hodgins's was similar to the corner store his mom had shopped near Clark Street. Only everything seemed bigger and more threatening. He also had the feeling that every eye in the store was watching him, wondering what a little boy was doing in here all by himself.

He looked up at a man behind the counter ringing up purchases, probably Mr. Hodgins. He was a tall man, slender except around the middle, and had a well-trimmed mustache. He wore a thick sweater under his white apron.

A stock boy stacked a fresh supply of White Rose green beans down the center aisle. Patrick almost walked right into him, his eyes so focused on his list. "Excuse me," Patrick said, backing up.

The stock boy smiled, and his thick glasses slid down his nose. "You're awfully young to be shopping on your own, aren't you? Your mom nearby?"

The question stung like a bee sting in Patrick's heart. He realized this had been the first day since his mom had died that he hadn't cried, and that made him feel guilty somehow.

"Is anything wrong?"

"I'm not here with my mom. I'm here with Mrs. Fortini."

"Mrs. Fortini? I know her. Big Italian lady." The stock boy looked around nervously, as though he'd said an improper thing. "I mean, she's really nice. My name's Harold, by the way."

"I'm Patrick. Mrs. Fortini's next door buying meat. She gave me this list and said to set the things on the counter till she came. She said Mr. Hodgins wouldn't mind."

"No, he won't. You need any help?"

"I might. I was looking for green beans."

Harold reached over and lifted a can off the shelf. "Here you go. White Rose. You can check one item off your list."

Patrick smiled as he took the can. He looked at the strange writing on top: ".15/10 pts." "What's this mean?"

"That's fifteen cents and ten points. Got any ration stamps with you?"

"No. That mean I can't buy it?"

"Do you have any money?"

"No."

"I'm sure Mrs. Fortini does. She told you just set them on the counter, right?"

"Right."

"She'll probably take care of the bill when she comes in. You might want to get yourself a basket over there by the door first. You've got quite a few things on your list."

"Thanks." Patrick took his can of beans and found the baskets. As he set the can inside, a strange sense of joy came over him. He was doing it. Shopping by himself. Just then, the door opened and he heard someone call his name. He turned and looked. He couldn't believe it. "Miss Townsend!" he cried.

He dropped his basket, and it crashed to the floor. Everyone watched as he ran and jumped into her arms.

∽

Katherine felt those quick tears forming in her eyes. She bent down and lifted Patrick up. He was hugging her so tight. "How are you, Patrick?" she said as he slid to the ground.

"Is my father home yet?"

Katherine tried to hide her sigh. "Not yet, but I was talking to a man this morning—an Air Force major—who said he would try to find something out today." The look on Patrick's face broke her heart. "Don't worry, Patrick. I promised I would get him home as fast as I could, and I will. How is your grandfather treating you?"

"Sometimes okay, I guess."

She could just imagine. *The boy's fine*, went through her head. She noticed a young red-haired man dressed in a white apron coming up to them.

"You his mom?" the young man said.

"No, just a friend." She didn't want to embarrass Patrick by revealing her official role. Besides, she was a friend.

"A relative of Mrs. Fortini?"

"Who?"

"He said he was with Mrs. Fortini. Isn't she at Ray's Meats?" he asked Patrick.

"Yes."

"That's right," said Katherine. "Your grandfather said his next-door neighbor brought you. She left you in the store alone?"

"It's okay," said Patrick. "I'm having fun. I just got my first thing. This can of beans." He walked over and picked up his basket and can. "Harold was helping me."

"Ray's is right next door," Harold said, giving her a look.

She knew that look, a more innocent version of Bernie Krebb's look. He looked down at her hands, as if searching for a wedding ring. She quickly walked over to Patrick before Harold asked her what time she got off work. "Well, Patrick," she said, bending down. "I can't stay too long today, but I wanted to come out and see for myself how you were doing." She talked quietly and turned her back to Harold as she spoke. He seemed to get the message and walked away.

"I'm glad you came. I missed you."

That smile. Those eyes. She wanted to take him in her arms again and make him her own. "I missed you too. That's why I came. You know, my boss didn't want me to. He wanted me to wait a few more days to give you and your grandfather some more time. But I wanted to see you."

His smile grew even wider. Then a frown. "He doesn't like me, and I don't know why."

"Your grandfather?"

Patrick nodded.

"I think he likes you, he just . . . I don't think he knows how to show it."

"He yelled at me yesterday, really loud. But I don't even know what I did that was wrong."

"Do you want me to talk to him? 'Cause I will."

Patrick thought for a minute. "I don't know. That might just get him madder."

"Has he hurt you? In any way?"

"Just in here," he said, pointing to his heart.

She felt a pain in her own heart. How could this man not see what a precious gift he was throwing away?

"It doesn't seem to matter what I do, he just doesn't like me. I need my dad to come home. That's all what I need."

He started to cry, and she pulled him close. "I'm going to bring him home, Patrick. As soon as I can. I'll keep calling those army people until they make him come home. But you know what? You haven't told me what you want for Christmas yet. It's only a few more days away. I'd like to get you a present, if it doesn't cost too much."

He pulled back and looked into her eyes. His smile was returning. "I know what I want most of all—except having my dad home, I mean."

"What is it?"

"It wouldn't cost anything, but I don't know how you could get it."

"Try me."

"It's something I saw in my grandfather's attic yesterday."

"Oh?"

"It's a wooden soldier. You know, the kind you carve with a knife. It's about this tall." He spread his hands about eighteen inches apart. "It's just sitting up there all dusty. It's not even finished. It doesn't have any feet yet, and it's not painted any colors."

"Have you asked your grandfather about it?"

"I started to on the attic stairs."

"What happened?"

"He grabbed it out of my hands and started yelling something about me being just like my dad. But it didn't sound like he thought that was good. I didn't understand him. He was so mad I just ran to my room."

"Well, I'll see what I can do. Is there anything else you want? Like something at a store? Something you heard about on the radio?"

"I'll think about it," he said.

The door opened behind them. Katherine turned to find a large Italian woman all dressed in black. "Patrick," she cried. "Are you all right?"

Katherine stood. "He's fine. Are you Mrs. Fortini?"

"Yes." She walked over to Patrick and put her arm around his shoulder.

"Hi, my name is Miss Townsend," she said, extending her hand. "I'm with Child Services. I've been with Patrick since

. . . well, I'm looking after him until we can get his father home from England."

"That's wonderful," said Mrs. Fortini. "Do you think it will be soon?"

"I hope so. Right, Patrick?"

He nodded.

"So how'd you make out on your first shopping trip?" Mrs. Fortini asked.

"I just got started, all I got was the beans."

"Well, we'll do the rest together, and then you'll be all trained for the next time."

"I better get going," Katherine said, looking at her watch. "I'm already overdue." Patrick ran over and gave her another hug. "I'll keep checking up on you, okay? And you call me if it gets too hard for you at your grandfather's."

"I'll keep an eye on that situation," said Mrs. Fortini. "I know what you're referring to."

Suddenly an image flashed into Katherine's mind. She remembered seeing a motto on the wall in Patrick's apartment in Clark Street, cross-stitched in a small golden frame. She bent down and took Patrick's chin in her hands. "Patrick, do you remember the Golden Rule?"

"I think so."

"What is it? What do you remember?"

"Do things for others that you want them to do for you."

"That's pretty close."

"My mom taught me. She made it into a picture thing she hung on the wall in our living room."

"I just remembered seeing it," said Katherine. "Why don't you try using the Golden Rule with your grandfather? See what happens."

"I'll try. I think my mom would want me to."

"Thanks for stopping by, Miss Townsend. A pleasure to meet you."

"Thank you for looking after Patrick for me, Mrs. Fortini. I feel a little better now about leaving him with . . . well. Do you have a phone?"

"I just got one a few months ago. What a wonderful thing."

"Could I call you sometime later today or tomorrow? I asked Patrick about a Christmas present, and he mentioned something about a wooden soldier in the attic."

"Oh my," said Mrs. Fortini.

"Is that bad?"

"You call me, and I'll explain. Let me write down my number." She handed Katherine a slip of folded paper, and Katherine gave her a business card in return.

Katherine gave Patrick another hug good-bye then walked back out into the cold. On the way toward her car, she vowed to double her efforts to find Patrick's father. She didn't care what Bernie Krebb said about getting personally involved. She was involved. If she lost her job over it, so be it. At least she could sleep well at night. And she could still keep seeing Patrick.

How bad could it be working in a factory, anyway?

&

When Katherine got back to her office, there was a message on her desk. It looked like Shirley O'Donnell's writing. Shirley worked in the cubicle next door. It said:

Major Jennings from the Air Force called. You spoke with him earlier today. Please return call right away. He said extremely urgent!

She couldn't believe he'd gotten back to her so quickly. Wouldn't it be great to finally have some good news for Patrick? She leaned over the cubicle and looked down at Shirley bent over her desk reading a file. "Shirley, you take this call for me?"

"What?"

"This is your handwriting, isn't it? When did Major Jennings call?"

"Three times since you left."

"Three times," Katherine repeated. She waited for some elaboration. "Did he say anything else?"

"Just what the note says."

"That's it?"

"Katherine . . ." She sounded a little annoyed.

"I'm sorry. This is important."

"Well, if it's important, sit down and call him back."

"Did he sound happy or sad to you?"

"I don't know."

"You don't know if he sounded happy or sad?"

"I guess I'd call it more like serious."

"You sure it wasn't just businesslike?"

"No, I'd say more like serious. Just call him, Kath. What are you getting so nervous about? What's it to you, anyway?"

"Nothing," said Katherine. "Thanks for taking the calls."

"No problem," she said, swiveling in her chair to face Katherine. "Thought I should tell you, though," she said quietly. "Krebb took notice of you coming in late from lunch, gave you the evil eye, and then . . . that other look."

"But I wasn't at lunch; I was on a call."

"Guess he didn't know. I said that's where you were."

"Thanks for covering for me."

"No problem."

Katherine sat at her desk, staring at the note. So Major Jennings had called three times, his voice a definite serious. She sighed heavily.

Would he call three times about good news?

Seventeen

"What'd you do with the boy?" Collins asked as he watched Mrs. Fortini marching in through the vestibule, holding two bags in her arms.

"I sold him to some gypsies. What do you think I did with him?" She rounded the corner and disappeared into the kitchen.

He closed the door. "Why I asked . . . I don't know. That Miss Townsend find you? You give him to her?"

"What a delightful young girl." Mrs. Fortini peeked her head out from the kitchen doorway. "You made her sound like some old hag."

"You still haven't told me what you did with the boy."

"Little boys like the snow, in case you don't remember. He asked if he could do something in the snow for a little while, and I said yes. You want me to call him in?"

Collins thought a moment and said, "I suppose it's all right. But he hasn't eaten lunch yet."

"After I put these things away, I'll make you both something."

Collins pulled his cigar out of his mouth. Either the cold, the wind, or the dampness had put it out. This front door has been opening way too much these last few days, Collins thought, and he didn't much like it. He walked over to the fireplace mantel to fetch a matchbook, listening to all the clanging and banging and rearranging going on in the kitchen. Mrs. Fortini was—her cooking qualities notwithstanding—such a loud woman. He knew this would happen once the boy came. In no time at all, his whole life would be turned upside down. Mrs. Fortini's wanting him to change this way, Miss Townsend wanting him to change that way. The boy asking for this, the boy asking for that. He walked over to the radiator to try and take some of the chill out of his bones.

He had to admit, though, all in all, the boy wasn't as bad as he could be. After he had gone off with Mrs. Fortini, Collins had gone upstairs to use the bathroom. The boy had made up his room once again, in fine military order. He cleaned up after himself pretty well in the kitchen too. Whatever else was wrong with the boy's mother, she seemed to instill some respect in him for other people's things.

Except for that wooden soldier in the attic.

Collins couldn't believe the boy's audacity, just picking something up that didn't belong to him and walking down the stairs with it. And of the thousands of oddball things lying around up there, why'd he have to fixate on that? Collins still wasn't over the pain just seeing that thing had dredged up in his heart.

Just another reason why the boy had to go. He was an instigator. At this stage in life, Collins didn't need or want instigation. He figured he deserved some peace and quiet, a little sameness and routine, if you please. That asking so much?

⁓

After Mrs. Fortini had finished putting away the food she had bought Collins and straightened up a bit, she made them both some lunch meat and cheese sandwiches. She'd have liked to stay awhile longer to look after Patrick, but she bought some things for herself at Ray's Meats that needed to go in her own icebox. She set the sandwiches on the dining room table along with two glasses of cold milk.

"Come and get it," she yelled to Collins as she walked into the living room. "I'll see to Patrick."

Collins got up out of his chair, moaning excessively. "Any change left from your shopping spree? Any ration coupons?"

"Next to my purse on the hutch," she said as she opened the front door. My, but it was cold. She stepped into the vestibule, hoping to spot Patrick without having to go outside.

She couldn't believe what she saw.

It nearly took her breath away. She had expected to find Patrick in the middle of building a snowman. "Hey, old man, get up. You have got to see this."

Collins had just set down to his sandwich. "What?"

"Come here, quick."

"I'm just getting ready to eat here. Can't you just tell me?"

"No, you have to see it." She heard his sigh all the way into the living room. She looked back outside at Patrick. From the first moment she had laid eyes on him, she had known he was special. Ida had told her about him over the years, always away from Collins's presence, fearing her secret relationship would be exposed and halted. Ida could only see Patrick through the occasional picture and letter sent to her by his mother, Elizabeth. Ida had never blamed Elizabeth for the feud and said she had quickly understood why Shawn had loved her so. Ida thought Elizabeth to be a most remarkable mom.

Now Mrs. Fortini could see why.

"What is it?" Collins mumbled as he stepped past her. "It's too blasted cold to leave this door open, woman."

"Oh, hush and look, look at your grandson." Collins turned and saw. She looked at his eyes, knowing he wouldn't be able to say what he truly felt about something like this. First she observed surprise. Then confusion as he processed the images. The confusion lingered a few seconds, replaced by a battle between cynicism and admiration. Admiration won out, resulting in a slight smile appearing on Collins's face. It was there just a moment, and she knew he'd never admit to it if she pointed it out. It was enough that she'd seen it for herself. His icy heart could still feel and care. It provided a pinch of hope.

"Who put him up to that?" Collins asked.

"No one." She turned and looked at Patrick again. He hadn't been doing any number of things a seven-year-old boy should be doing in the snow. Somewhere he'd gotten hold of a snow shovel. He had the whole walkway cleared from the front door to the driveway, and was presently digging a narrow walk through the driveway toward the street. His cheeks were blood red. He was obviously exhausted, but he kept at it. One shovelful at a time.

"You better call him in," Collins said, stepping back into the living room. "He's going to turn up sick he stays out there."

She opened the door. "Patrick, you're doing a wonderful job." He stopped and looked up, his face all smiles and pride. "Why don't you take a break? I've made your lunch. Would you like some hot cocoa with it?"

"Sure would," Patrick said, letting the shovel drop. He walked up into the vestibule, and she helped him out of his wet clothes.

"We're going to have to buy you a man's gloves," she said as she yanked off his mittens. "These are soaked."

Patrick walked over and stood by the radiator. He looked

at his grandfather, already back at the table, eating his sandwich, reading the sports page. She noted the discouragement on Patrick's face. She bent down and whispered in his ear, "He saw it, Patrick."

"He did?" Patrick whispered back.

"And he smiled."

"Really?"

"Saw it myself."

Patrick walked toward the dining room at a lively step. "I am so hungry."

"You should be after all that work. Right, Mr. Collins?"

"What?"

"Hard work makes a man hungry, right?"

"Hard work never hurt a soul," he said without looking up.

Patrick took his seat at the table and began devouring his sandwich.

"You finish eating, and I'll start that cocoa," Mrs. Fortini said.

"Cocoa," Collins mumbled. "You wasted my blue stamps on cocoa?"

"Oh, hush up and finish your sandwich."

As she walked past Collins, she looked back at Patrick and winked.

Eighteen

Her frustration and anxiety was growing by the minute.

In between a handful of other tasks, Katherine had called Major Jennings four times over the last two hours but was unable to reach him. It didn't mean anything, she kept telling herself. She should stop calling and trust her message would get through. He'd call back today. He wouldn't make her wait all night.

Bernie Krebb walked by her cubicle on his way to his office and glared down at her, making her suddenly aware she was sitting there doing nothing. She picked up the telephone, faking a call. Her eyes scrambled for something to do. She noticed a slip of paper sticking out of her purse. It was Mrs. Fortini's phone number. As the telephone began to ring on the other end, Krebb turned his attention elsewhere.

"Hello?"

"Mrs. Fortini? This is Miss Townsend from Child Services. We met a few hours ago at the grocery store. I was there seeing Patrick."

"I remember. How are you?"

"I'm fine, thanks. And I want to thank you again for looking after Patrick. I didn't really want to leave him there with his grandfather, but I had no choice. I'm sorry. I shouldn't have said that."

"No need, Miss Townsend. Our Mr. Collins is . . . well, a very difficult man. This we all know. I've lived next door for years. His wife and I were best friends. He wasn't always this way. Well, not always as much this way."

"Do you know what he has against Patrick? I don't understand why he treats him so coldly. He's probably the finest little boy I've—"

"It's not Patrick. Mr. Collins and Patrick's father had a falling-out years ago. They haven't said hardly a word to each other since before Patrick was born."

"What's it all about? You don't have to get into this if you're uncomfortable—"

"No, that's all right. Ida tried to explain it to me, but she was a loyal wife. Whenever I asked questions, her answers were always very guarded. She did say there were some issues that divided them, some harsh words had been said, and now each was waiting for the other to relent and apologize. But both were too stubborn to ever do that, so the stalemate goes on. I thought for sure it would end when Patrick was born, and then Ida passed away, and here we are some years later and it's still going on." She paused a moment, then said, "Bitterness is a terrible thing."

"Could I ask you about something else? When I saw Patrick at the store, I asked if there was something I could get him for Christmas. I was expecting him to say something like a rifle or a toy car, but he wanted something very unusual."

"The wooden soldier in Mr. Collins's attic?"

"Yes. Patrick said his grandfather yanked it out of his hands after he'd found it yesterday and yelled at him."

"I'm surprised that's all he did."

"What's all this about? Patrick said it was some kind of hand-carved thing."

"It's an odd thing. To look at Mr. Collins and listen to him, he seems incapable of anything artistic or creative. But he's really quite talented when it comes to wood. He made the wooden soldier years ago. I don't think he's made anything else since. Ida showed it to me once. It's not like the Nutcracker or some childish toy; it's much more realistic. I think he made it after some hero from the First World War. But . . . he gave up before he finished it."

"Why?"

"From what Ida said, he was making it for Shawn. Back when they were just starting to have their problems. Shawn was away at school. I think it was supposed to be a surprise Christmas present, a way to patch things up. But then Shawn met Elizabeth, and he didn't come home that year. Mr. Collins stopped working on it. Ida said he left it out for a while but got sick of looking at it. She said he seemed to treat it almost like a symbol of their animosity. One day he said something like, 'All the hours I spent carving this thing . . . just a waste of time, like all the years I spent raising that boy.' And walked it up to the attic and she never saw it again, except at Christmas when she'd go up to get the decorations."

"Of all the things for Patrick to focus on," Katherine said.

"I don't see him ever agreeing to letting Patrick have it," said Mrs. Fortini.

"I'd ask him, but he can't stand me."

"He doesn't think too highly of me, either," Mrs. Fortini said. "But I'd be willing to give it a try."

"I don't want to get you in any trouble."

"I'm always in trouble with him," she said. They both laughed.

Out of the corner of Katherine's eye, she noticed a hand waving off to the side. She looked up to see Shirley O'Donnell leaning over her cubicle. "Excuse me, Mrs. Fortini." Katherine covered the mouthpiece with her hand. "What is it?" she whispered.

"It's him," Shirley whispered back. "Line two."

"Who?"

"That major you been trying to reach. He's on line two."

Katherine's heart started pounding. "Okay, tell him I'll be right there." She took her hand off the mouthpiece. "Mrs. Fortini, I'm sorry. I've gotta go. Got a long-distance phone call I've gotta take." She was about to tell her who it was but changed her mind.

"That's all right. It's been nice talking to you. I'll do what I can with that old goat about the wooden soldier."

"Thanks, good-bye." She hung up the phone and turned in her chair very slowly. Shirley made a face. "Okay, Shirley. I'm ready."

"You are so ridiculous. Just pick up the phone. What's the big deal?"

Shirley was right. What was the big deal? She picked up line two. She looked at her hand; it was shaking. She was being ridiculous. But . . . it was a big deal. "Hello, Major Jennings. Thanks for returning my call."

Nineteen

Mrs. Fortini walked carefully down the sidewalk toward Collins's house. Patrick was hard at work finishing the driveway. The sun had already begun to descend, covering half the street in shadows. A chilly wind blew across the street, whipping a mist of snow into the air, wide enough to douse them both before it died away. The cold went right through her overcoat, but she noticed Patrick hardly broke his stride. One shovel after another.

"It looks wonderful, Patrick," she yelled as she turned into the driveway. "See? I can walk right down it now without getting any snow on my boots."

"You like it?" He stuck the shovel in a sidewall of snow and looked up at her.

"It's wonderful. Looks like you're almost done. But it's getting colder. I'm not sure you should be out here much longer."

He pointed to the far edge of the sidewalk. "Can I stop when I reach there?"

"Might be better to finish tomorrow."

He looked at the remaining distance. "Tomorrow's Sunday. Can I do this on Sunday?"

"That's right, the Lord's Day . . . I don't know, what did your mommy teach you?"

"I can't remember. Seems like I heard something about it."

"Well, don't worry about it now. I just don't want you to catch cold. The sun's going down." She walked past him toward Collins's front door, patting his hat.

"I'll just do a few more feet, then I'll quit. I want to make it nice and even."

She turned back toward the house in time to catch Collins peeking through the front curtains. He quickly backed away.

Collins hurried over to the cardboard box delivered yesterday and quickly put the little boxful of letters back in their place and closed the flaps. The commotion outside had put a quick end to his exploration. All day long the letters had been tempting him, and he had resisted. At first, he refused to acknowledge the interest. But it reached a point where it was futile to pretend otherwise. He hated this. It wasn't like him. But he felt like he had to know more.

So in a way, he was glad for the interruption. He didn't have a chance to read even a single one, and it was probably just as well.

Getting caught by Mrs. Fortini was unacceptable. He heard the outer vestibule door open and close with a clang. Such a noisy woman. Collins quickly took his place in his chair, even picked up the sports page to cover his tracks. Then the knock at the door.

Collins waited a moment, not wanting her to think he was in any hurry. Somehow the boy's presence had given Mrs. Fortini the authority to burst into his life whenever she pleased. "I'm coming," he yelled. She banged again. "Hold your horses."

As he opened the door, she was taking off her boots. Great, he thought. She planned to make more of this than a doorway chat. "What do you want now?"

"Good evening to you too," she said.

Collins stepped out of the way to let her through.

"I just want to talk to you about something, and I don't want you to listen in a snippety mood."

"I don't even know what a snippety mood is."

"It's your normal mood."

"Is this really necessary?"

"I'm sorry, am I interrupting something important?"

Collins sighed. No matter how hard he tried, there was no intimidating this woman. No wonder her husband had departed this world early.

She walked in and took a seat on the sofa closest to his chair. "Come over here and have a seat. This won't take but a minute."

He dutifully obeyed, halting momentarily in silent protest before sitting. "All right, what's this about?" He knew it must have something to do with the boy.

"Have you thought about what you're going to do for Christmas? What you're going to get Patrick? It's just a few days away."

"His father should be here before then."

"What difference does that make? Shawn comes home and somehow that means you can't get your grandson a Christmas present?"

The thought had never entered his mind. "You came all the way over here like there was some serious thing to talk about."

"This is serious. Christmas is important, you old Scrooge. To most people, anyway. And to kids especially. And for Patrick, this year is going to be especially difficult—"

"I don't need you telling me this."

"Yes, you do, if you're not thinking about it on your own. And obviously you're not."

Collins reached for his cigar. It might just be time to blow a big puff in her direction. Either that or get mad enough to start swearing, and he liked her tomato juice too much to risk that. He relit the cigar, then puffed heavily to secure the burn. She coughed as the smoke dissipated about her head.

"That's not going to work, old man. Not this time. Don't you care about Patrick?"

"I took him in, didn't I? Didn't have to. That Townsend woman said she'd take him if I wanted."

"Ian . . . he's your grandson. He's just lost his mother. His father is two thousand miles away. It's Christmastime."

She had never called him by his first name. It was always Mr. Collins. And she was always Mrs. Fortini. And he rather preferred it that way. And she was talking way too kindly just now. He preferred the loud Italian version more.

"Are you listening?"

"Yes, he's my grandson. I'm aware of that."

"You weren't listening."

"Would you just get to the point?"

"You need to give him a Christmas present. Something special, something he'll remember."

"I don't know what a little boy wants."

"There's a simple solution to that. You could ask him."

Collins sighed loudly through his teeth. Another smoke cloud drifted toward Mrs. Fortini, then broke apart.

She coughed once, then continued. "I think I already know something you could give him, and it wouldn't cost you a red cent."

Collins could see there was no cutting this lecture short

without at least a pretense of cooperation. "All right, what is it?"

Mrs. Fortini straightened back up in her seat. "Remember that old wooden soldier you carved many years ago? It's just sitting up there in your attic. I happen to know—"

"What?" Collins yelled, rising to his feet.

Mrs. Fortini leaned back in her chair. "Don't get upset."

"I see what's going on here. The boy put you up to this, didn't he?" In the commotion, no one heard the vestibule door open and close.

"He did no such thing. He has no idea—"

"So that's it then . . . you tell him to go outside and shovel the sidewalk to butter me up, then you come in here to do his dirty work. Well, it's not going to work."

"You old fool." She stood in front of him now. "That's not what happened at all."

"I told him yesterday he had no business laying a hand on that thing. He's got no rights to it and no right sending you in here to ask me about it."

"He didn't send me in here—"

Collins walked into the dining room and leaned on the table, facing away from her. "I should have thrown that stupid thing out a long time ago. It's been nothing but trouble." He turned and said, "You can just walk right back out there and tell him his little scheme didn't work. I don't care if he—" His finger was jabbing the air in her direction when he noticed the front door standing open and Patrick standing there. Mrs. Fortini turned and saw Patrick too.

Patrick let his coat fall to the floor and ran up the stairs, tears streaming down his face.

Mrs. Fortini got up without saying a word. She picked up Patrick's coat and hung it up, then put on her own. "You are really something," she said. "Patrick shoveled your stupid sidewalk all by himself, without being asked or told. And we never once talked about the wooden soldier." She walked out to the vestibule, put on her boots, and headed out the door without looking back.

I don't need all this, Collins thought as the door closed. *I don't need any of it.*

༄

Katherine hadn't uttered a word in thirty minutes. She just sat there, her eyes fixed on a stapler. She didn't see it or anything else on her desk. She was barely in the room, her mind almost in a state of paralysis. Thoughts tried to form, but emotions ruled the moment.

Most of the other girls had gone home already. Bernie Krebb had said good night ten minutes ago as he walked by, but she didn't hear. It was for times just like these that the agency had created the policy of keeping client relationships objective and impersonal. She knew that now. Why did she leave herself open for this kind of pain?

How could she face Patrick now with this news?

Twenty

As upset as he was by his grandfather's harsh words, Patrick didn't cry very much this time. Instead, he got angry.

After just a few minutes, he sat up in his bed. He glanced at his parents' smiling picture on the dresser. But he wasn't smiling back. He stood up and looked out the window, his arms folded. "Nothing I do is right with him. Nothing I do could ever make him nice. Now I know why we never came here to visit. I hate—"

But he couldn't say it.

As he turned back toward the bed, he caught a glimpse of his mother's eyes. "You should never hate anyone," he remembered her saying, just after he'd gotten in a fight with an older boy and said he hated him. "Where would we be if God hated us every time we did something wrong?" Then she cupped his chin softly in her palm. "We can't treat people one way and expect God to treat us another . . . right?" He knew she was right, both then and now. But he didn't want to think about it anymore.

He wanted to run away. If only he had someplace to go.

He decided to go next door to Mrs. Fortini's house. At least it was someplace else. He wouldn't ask permission; he would just do it, just get up and go. He opened the door and peeked into the hallway. It was empty. He stepped out, his ears reaching for every room of the house. He stepped lightly down the steps, careful to avoid the squeaky ones.

Suddenly, a toilet flushed behind him, then a knob turned. Only a few moments to make his escape. He ran down the remaining stairs, grabbed his coat from the floor, and made his way to the vestibule. He put on his coat and boots as he stepped out into the cold, pulling the wet mittens from his pockets. He finished the buttons halfway down the driveway.

The sun was nearly gone now, the sky shifting to a deep navy blue. Patrick stopped just a moment to look back at the job he'd done on the driveway, then his eyes drifted up toward the house. All the other homes on the street already had their Christmas lights on, but not his grandfather's. His house was cloaked in dark shadows.

Why did Patrick have to be at this house?

A few steps later he was at Mrs. Fortini's driveway, but as he turned he slipped face-first on a thin layer of ice, plunging him into a snowbank. He dug the snow out of his eyes and picked himself up, brushed off his coat. He took shorter steps the rest of the way. He knocked softly on the door, afraid to make any noise that would alert his grandfather. As he waited, he noticed two stars hanging in her front window, one blue, the other gold. His mother had told him what the stars meant. The gold star must be Frankie's, he thought.

"Patrick," Mrs. Fortini said loudly. "Come in, come in. What are you doing here?"

Patrick looked into her eyes, relieved to see a gentle smile. He collapsed into the folds of her apron as she hugged him and rubbed his head. "Let's get these wet clothes off. How'd you get so much snow on your face? One of those older boys hit you with a snowball?" She stepped out onto the porch and gave a menacing look up and down the street.

"I just fell."

He had never been here, but as he looked around, he was surprised at how familiar the rooms were. Then he realized it was just like his grandfather's place, only the opposite. It also had more furniture and throw rugs down the hall and into the dining room. The entire room smelled of things baking and thick perfume. Why couldn't he live here while he waited for his father to come home?

"You take off the coat and boots and put them on the towel by the door," she said as she closed the front door. "Warm yourself up by the radiator a few minutes. I'll get you a little snack, but nothing too heavy so close to dinner."

Patrick did what she asked. As he walked toward the radiator, he was captivated by three framed photographs propped on a dark wooden table. The center one showed two young men smiling, leaning up against a black car, waving at the camera. The man on the left was a sailor, the other a soldier. On either side of this picture were photos of each man by himself, from their shoulders up, still in uniform. Must be her sons, he thought.

The sailor must be Frankie, the one who died at Pearl Harbor. He could see Mrs. Fortini's smile in his face. Frankie looked so alive when this picture was taken, thought Patrick, like he would always be alive, like he was alive right now. But he was not.

Then he remembered his talk with Mrs. Fortini by the cemetery. Frankie was gone . . . but he was still alive. Alive but very far away. He wondered what good was it if you couldn't touch them or see their eyes blink, their smiles move, or their heads turn when you talked to them. He wondered if Mrs. Fortini ever talked to Frankie's picture. He'd have to tell her how much it helped him.

"I see you've noticed my boys. Remember I told you about my Frankie?"

"The sailor, right?"

"That's right. He's in heaven now. Every day I pray for his brother Dominic to be safe. He's in England where your father is."

"Is he a bomber pilot?"

"Thank goodness, no," she said, then seemed to regret it. "He is just a mechanic. He fixes planes. Dominic was always good with engines and tools."

"Maybe he works on my father's plane."

"Maybe," she said. "Here, sit down and have a cookie, but only one. The milk is fresh, just came this morning."

The oatmeal cookie was delicious, and the milk made the experience complete. His smile grew as he looked at all her Christmas decorations. He'd almost forgotten it was Christmastime. There was a large nativity scene spread across a small table by the window. Holly branches covered the arches of each doorway. Scattered on every ledge and shelf were Santas, angels, and elves. "Are you getting a tree?" he asked.

"Of course. What would Christmas be without a tree? A nice man across the street, Mr. Murphy, is getting one for me on Christmas Eve. If you're still here, you can help me set it up. Would you like that?"

"Would I."

"You could come over the day before and help me make some new ornaments."

"You make 'em?"

"Since the war, they haven't been selling any new ones, so each year I make a few new ones to replace the ones that break. It'll be fun. We'll roll up pieces of cardboard into little balls and wrap tinfoil around them. Then I've got some pinecones we could paint."

"I would like that." He got up and walked his plate and glass out to the sink.

"What a gentleman," she said.

"Mrs. Fortini? What are all those things poking out of the snow?" Patrick asked, looking out the back window.

Mrs. Fortini came and stood behind him. "Those? That's the top of my little fence."

"That's only how big your yard is? My grandfather's yard is way bigger."

"No, silly. That's not my whole backyard. It's my Victory Garden. See how the posts are shaped like a V? Do you know what a Victory Garden is?"

"We didn't have any backyards on Clark Street."

"It's a way of helping with the war. People with yards are supposed to grow as much food as we can so the farmers can give more food to the soldiers."

Patrick looked again. He still couldn't make out the V.

"Last spring I grew all sorts of things. Tomatoes, carrots, zucchini. I had to put a fence around it to keep the dogs out." She walked to the sink and rinsed off the plates, then they walked back to the living room.

"I'll ask your grandfather then."

"Ask him what?"

"Ask him if you can help me decorate my tree in a few days. How long did he say you could visit?"

Patrick looked down at the rug. He didn't want to answer.

"He doesn't know you're here?"

"I was afraid he would say no. But I had to see you." He looked up.

After a pause, she said, "That's all right, Patrick. But we'll need to get you back over there somehow. Maybe he doesn't know you've left yet. Let's get your coat on."

⁓

It was his last telegram of the day. The Western Union driver waited at the traffic light, glancing down at the map, trying to ignore the stares. The curious passersby. Drivers and passengers in cars throughout the intersection. He turned right onto Clifton Ave., double-checking the map.

The weatherman had predicted more snow to hit later that evening. The wind was expected to pick up too, bringing with it almost blizzardlike conditions. Hopefully, he'd get this last telegram out and be back home before the storm hit.

Here was the next street. He glanced at the map once more as he turned the wheel. That's the one, he thought, Chestnut Street. He hoped this last telegram might bring good news. Every now and then it happened: a son missing in action had been found safe; a son missing and presumed dead had been identified as a POW. Moments like these were the only bright spots in his day.

He looked down at the name above the address:

Mr. Ian Collins.

Twenty-One

He didn't even feel the biting cold anymore. Standing there in the vestibule, Ian Collins read the words but could not register their meaning. Western Union Telegram. What was he holding?

"Have a good evening, sir," the young man said nervously as he backed out of the doorway. "Merry Christmas," he said as he turned and walked away.

Collins heard the door latch click. He looked up and noticed several neighbors standing on their porches, others looking out their windows. Two women had stopped on the sidewalk a few doors down and turned. Vultures, he thought, every last one of them. None of them liked him, not even when Ida was here. He gave them each his meanest glare until, one by one, they pulled back into their homes.

He backed into the living room and slammed the front door. *It's probably just a note from Shawn telling me when he'll be home*, Collins thought. *Shawn wouldn't call; he wouldn't want to talk in person; he'd send a telegram. That's all this is. Wrote to tell me when he'd be in to get the boy.* Still, the hand holding the telegram trembled. He tried to make it stop, but it wouldn't mind. He shuffled toward his chair, staring down at the envelope. He sat, then stood up again, thinking a person should read a telegram standing.

He took a deep breath, tore it open.

Before he read the first line, he got a feeling something was missing. He scanned the ashtrays in the living room until he saw it in the pewter tray on the fireplace mantel. He hurried over and shoved the cigar in his mouth. He remained standing as he slid the yellow telegram out of the envelope and read the first line. His stomach tensed up; he felt his heart beating in his temples.

The telegram wasn't from Shawn. It was about him.

```
PAL37 49 GOVT=WUX WASHINGTON DC DEC 22 112P
MR IAN COLLINS=235 CHESTNUT ST=
THE SECRETARY OF WAR HAS ASKED ME TO EXPRESS
   HIS DEEP REGRET THAT YOUR SON CAPT SHAWN
   COLLINS WAS REPORTED MISSING IN ACTION
   DEFENDING HIS COUNTRY OVER GERMANY
A CONFIRMING LETTER FOLLOWS=
E F WITSELL ACTING THE ADJUTANT GENERAL OF
   THE ARMY.
```

MISSING IN ACTION.

The words repeated over and over in his mind, finally sinking in at about the fifth revolution. Collins was not an emotional man, save for his anger. But he felt like a man standing too close to a rising stream and the ledge beneath his feet just gave way. He blinked back tears that suddenly appeared, literally willing them away. *It says "Missing in Action,"* he thought, *not "Killed in Action." There's no reason to assume Shawn is dead. Missing means missing. It doesn't mean—*

Suddenly a picture of a black-and-white newsreel began to replay in his mind.

Collins was back in time two weeks ago, before the boy had arrived. He had just slipped into the Clifton Theater on a Saturday afternoon, taking a seat in the back row. He didn't know what movie was playing and didn't care. He had simply walked past the shops bordering the theater in search of a deli sandwich. He looked up and saw the word "Newsreels" at the bottom of the movie marquee.

Here the war had been raging for two full years and he still hadn't seen any newsreels. He knew the air war over Germany was in full bloom. Allied planes were being sent across the English Channel almost every day. He knew Shawn was on some of those missions. Shawn's plane was dropping some of those bombs. Curiosity got the better of him. The next thing he knew, Collins was standing in line. Once inside, he walked past the lines at the concession stand. In a few minutes, the lights dimmed and the newsreel began, a Fox Movietone production.

The sights astounded him, far more gripping than he'd expected. He watched ship convoys, one after the other, helplessly attacked by German U-boats. He'd never seen such a thing. The stricken vessels sank so quickly, like bathtub toys, tossing sailors into the frigid waters.

The scene shifted.

Allied destroyers rose and fell in the rough Pacific waves. Battleships blasted their huge guns. The center of a Japanese ship erupted like a volcano, then split in two, sending both halves quickly to the bottom.

The scene shifted again.

Air Force generals pored over battle maps, rubbing their chins, pointing to selected targets. Collins's hands tensed around the armrests at the next scene: ground crews loaded bombs onto B-17s and B-24s. The bombers taxied out to runways and slowly lifted off the tarmac. Hundreds of planes gathered in the skies, majestic contrails streaming behind them. Then Collins realized . . . Shawn was in one of those planes. Could he have just seen his plane in the film?

The scene shifted again, now inside one of the planes.

Gunners dressed like Eskimos wrestled with machine guns as spent shell casings hit the floor. The camera moved outside, into the skies. The film vibrated violently, then focused on little black specks that quickly became Nazi fighter planes darting through the bombers.

Collins tensed again as one Allied bomber, smoke pouring from two engines, fell off to one side then began spinning wildly out of control. The camera followed its descent. Collins didn't see any parachutes. From his mechanical background, he understood a little bit about what was going on. Those poor young men, he thought, stuck inside a spinning airplane, aware they were going down, probably screaming in terror, pinned by centrifugal force against the fuselage wall. They had almost no chance of escape.

Collins witnessed two more bombers going down. Between the three planes, he counted only four parachutes. He'd read an article in *Look* magazine that said each bomber carried ten men. He quickly did the math. That meant four men had survived out of thirty that went down . . . in just those few minutes.

Only four . . . out of thirty.

Collins stood there now in his living room, holding the telegram. Five words seemed to magnify on the page:

MISSING IN ACTION OVER GERMANY.

Shawn's plane had been shot down, just like those planes in the newsreel. That same *Look* article said the pilots were usually the last to get out alive. They kept the planes flying steady until the others could bail out. Shawn would have done that, Collins thought. He would have done his duty to the end.

These thoughts and images became an arrow pointing in one inevitable direction—Shawn wasn't missing; he was dead. It was that simple. The confirming letter to follow would only confirm that fact, the army's way of letting a family down easy.

He set the telegram on the end table next to his ashtray. He was sitting now, though he didn't remember doing so. He looked at the floor; at some point, his cigar had fallen from his mouth. Tears began to pour down his face. He tried holding them back, then wiping them away, but there was no stopping them. He looked up at the door, then the windows, as if someone might see.

He finally gave up, buried his face in his hands, and let the tears flow. His whole body erupted into heaving sobs.

"Shawn," he cried. "My boy. My poor boy."

Twenty-Two

Katherine Townsend had cried nonstop since receiving the call from Major Jennings that afternoon. A few co-workers took notice. Several called out as she ran through the halls, asking if everything was okay, was there anything they could do. She had never been so grateful to find the elevator empty.

She had promised Patrick she'd bring his father home safe, and soon. Now she had hope of neither. Her only hope now was that she would beat the Western Union man.

As she drove along, she thought about the phone call. Major Jennings reminded her that Patrick's father was reported only as missing in action. When she had pressed for his opinion on his chances of being found alive, a long, agonizing pause followed. "We can always hope" was all he'd said. She had to convince the elder Collins not to say anything to Patrick as long as there was a shred of hope his father would be found alive. Perhaps even someone as stubborn as he could see the wisdom in that.

The snow began to fall as she turned right onto Clifton Avenue. It was coming down heavily, suggesting a brewing storm. Her car didn't have snow tires or chains. She'd have to watch the time so she could make it back before the roads became too difficult to manage. As she approached Chestnut Street, her heart sank even deeper in its despair. At the intersection, a Western Union truck had just turned going in the opposite direction.

She was too late.

⟡

Mrs. Fortini had just finished putting on her black coat, gloves, and boots. She reached for her fur hat on the hook by the front door and looked out the window. The storm the weathermen had predicted had started. At least twelve to fourteen inches with drifts up to two feet. With the snow already laying on the ground, it would make getting around very difficult over the next few days. "You need help with your boots, Patrick?"

"No, I got 'em."

"It's starting to snow. We better hurry."

"Really?" He got right up and limped to the window, dragging his unlatched boot. "Wow. You think it will snow all the way to Christmas?"

"It better not. We'll be buried alive. C'mon, let me help you with that boot."

They made their way out into the cold, carefully holding onto the rail as they descended the steps. The wind whipped the snowflakes into their faces. "It hurts," Patrick yelled.

"Come here," Mrs. Fortini shouted over the wind, pulling Patrick close to her side. They reached the end of her driveway. She threw her scarf across her face and eyed the distance left to travel. "I think we should head back to the house until this wind dies down a bit." She was nervous about covering the icy sidewalk, what with the wind and a frightened little boy clinging to her leg. "I can call your grandfather from the house," she said as she turned around. Patrick offered no objections.

Just then she looked down the street and noticed a truck trying to turn right at the intersection, its tires spinning in the sleet. She thought she saw the familiar Western Union emblem on the side panel as it cleared the curb. Instantly she remembered that terrible day she got her telegram about Frankie.

As she watched the truck disappear, she said a prayer for whatever family in the neighborhood might be receiving bad news this evening. This was her way of extinguishing sad memories before they unraveled too far.

So far, it hadn't even occurred to Ian Collins that Patrick might not be in the house. The shock from the telegram still ruled the moment. His tears had dried temporarily, leaving him with puffy eyes. A heaviness, deeper than the heaviness that had visited him after Ida died, descended upon him.

His normal shuffle across the living room rug had slowed to a crawl. Presently, he was scouring the dining room pantry for a bottle of whiskey he knew he'd stashed somewhere for special occasions. It had never been opened. He certainly didn't consider this occasion special. He simply wanted relief, actually to get drunk, and that as quickly as possible.

His trembling hands bumped a glass bottle of cooking oil. It tumbled from the shelf and shattered on the wooden floor. He swore as he heard the crash, looked down for a moment, but continued fingering the upper shelves in search of his prize. He finally located the whiskey bottle and carefully lifted it from its hold. He heard a loud pounding on the door and wondered why someone would be knocking so rudely. He sighed as he turned from his mission and stepped carefully over the puddle of broken glass and oil.

He suspected it to be Mrs. Fortini. He nervously wiped his eyes and stretched his face in a variety of exercises, hoping to achieve a normal expression. He looked out the front window and groaned. "Not now."

It was that nosey Townsend woman.

Twenty-Three

As she looked into Collins's eyes, Katherine knew instantly he had heard the news about Shawn. "May I come in?" Katherine asked. Collins backed up a few steps but did not reply. Her eyes instantly fell upon the telegram lying on the end table, but she pretended not to see. "That's some storm we got brewing," she said.

"I suppose," he said in a voice uncharacteristically subdued.

"Is Patrick here?"

"Upstairs in his room. Why?"

"I don't want him to hear what I have to say. Could we go into the dining room?"

Collins didn't answer; he just moved in that direction. They came upon the oil spill. "Had a little accident. Watch your step."

Katherine looked at the mess, then the whiskey bottle on the hutch, instantly understanding what had occurred. *Can't fault him for that,* she thought, wondering if a stiff drink wouldn't help her cope right now with her own growing depression. She quickly took her eyes off the bottle and focused on Collins's face. "I saw the Western Union truck pulling away as I came on your street. I suppose he was here?"

Collins nodded then looked away.

Katherine actually felt sorrow for the old man. "I spoke with an Air Force major named Jennings. He said Shawn was just listed as missing in action."

"I know."

"There's always hope," she offered.

Collins sighed in reply, then said, "What did you want to discuss?"

Katherine looked up at the stairway. "Like I said, missing in action means there's hope Patrick's father will still be found."

"I'd say the chances of that are slim," he said with an edge.

"You don't know that."

"No, I don't."

"Patrick is expecting him home any day."

"So was I."

"We're going to have to think of something to say. Patrick would be devastated by this news, especially coming on the heels of losing his mother. I was hoping you'd feel the same way."

"What are you getting at?"

"I don't think we should tell him. Not as long as he's just listed as missing." Collins seemed lost in thought, as though unable to process what she said. "We can tell him there's been a delay, buy us some time until we learn more about the situation."

"Madam, I'm not prepared to be the caretaker of a little boy. I've got my own life to worry about. You said it would just be for a week or two."

"What?"

"For all we know, my son could be dead. And if by some

miracle he survived being shot down, that means he's a POW in Nazi Germany . . . for who knows how long?"

Katherine couldn't believe what she was hearing. "So what are you saying?"

"I don't know what I'm saying. I'm saying I'm not ready for this. I'm too old for this—"

"Keep your voice down."

"Don't scold me in my own house."

"Patrick will hear."

"Then let him hear. He's going to find out soon enough anyway."

"Mr. Collins!"

"Look, I didn't ask for this—for any of this." Tears welled up in his eyes. "He's not a bad boy. But I'm just not up to all this. I've just found out my own boy is gone, and I—"

"He's just missing, Mr. Collins. He's not gone."

"Call it what you will. He was going to be home any day, and now . . . who knows? I can't keep this up, you're going to have to . . ." His voice tapered off as he turned his back to her and wiped his tears away.

She knew he was just releasing emotions. She couldn't imagine the volcanic explosion that would erupt if someone as self-centered and bottled up as Ian Collins finally let it all go. She didn't want to be around when that happened. More importantly, she didn't want Patrick to be around for it either. This might be just the thing to . . . "Mr. Collins." She tried to keep an even tone. "If you'd like, I could arrange to take Patrick with me. At least until we find out more about his father's situation."

"I don't know," he said, facing her again, trying to act as though he hadn't been crying.

"You need some time to deal with your grief. And with all due respect, Patrick needs to be shielded from it."

"What are you suggesting?"

"I don't have the forms with me right now, but I could write out a reasonable release form freehand. You could sign it, and I could take Patrick off your hands. Tonight."

A new expression seemed to form on his face, in his eyes. The steely, controlling Collins appeared to be regrouping.

"I'm sorry, I shouldn't be acting this way," he said, all emotion gone from his voice. "It's really not like me. I've got a duty here. The boy's family, maybe all I've got. Wouldn't be right to turn my back on him, no matter how I feel."

"I wouldn't call it turning my back on him. You just need a little time."

"I've had my little time right here with you. I'll be fine."

"Mr. Collins, I don't think that's wise."

"You don't, you being the fountain of wisdom and all."

"I'm not trying to insult you, sir; I'm just thinking of Patrick. I think it would be best if—"

"You think it would be best. Well, you're not in charge here, little lady. You had your say. I think it's time for you to leave." He started walking toward the front door.

Katherine stood her ground in the dining room. "Mr. Collins, you're not being rational. You're not putting Patrick's needs ahead of your own—this stubborn, Irish sense of duty."

"And you're not trying to insult me?" he asked, opening the front door. "If you don't mind, you're letting the cold in."

She stormed into the living room. She had no recourse, not now, anyway. "I'll go for now, sir. But I'll be back. I think I can convince my superiors that Patrick deserves better than this."

She walked right past him into the frigid vestibule. She turned to say something, but he slammed the door in her face. As she stepped into the icy wind, she scolded herself for losing her composure. Without Collins's consent, it would be a tough sell to free Patrick from his grasp. The car door creaked loudly as it opened, and the wind blew it shut.

The storm was definitely getting worse.

As she turned the car on, she began to think through her options. The easiest thing would be if Patrick would ask to be taken away on his own. But how could she get him to do that without appearing to be coached? With Collins opposing it, a judge would certainly take Patrick aside to make sure the decision was his own. First, she would try to explain the situation to her superiors, fill out a report requesting he be removed for his own good. She would volunteer to take him in. At least until after Christmas. That would remove the obstacle of finding him a suitable place with such short notice.

As she put the car in gear, a sinking depression began to mingle with her rage. A picture of Bernie Krebb's face came into view. There was no way he would back her on this.

She really was in the wrong line of work.

Twenty-Four

Back inside her home, Mrs. Fortini had just managed to pry
loose her left boot. Her feet ached from the chill. Patrick, still
fully covered in his winter gear, was standing by the living
room window, admiring the snow. Suddenly Patrick yelled,
startling her. "Miss Townsend!" He looked briefly at Mrs.
Fortini. "It's Miss Townsend's car; she's next door." He ran
out the front door.

"What? Patrick? Patrick, wait!"

"Miss Townsend," he yelled. "Over here. I'm over here."
She didn't seem to hear him, his voice swallowed by the wind.
He ran down the porch stairs, slipping on the third one.
It threw him headlong into the snow. He didn't care. He
picked himself up, brushing off the snow, and ran down the
driveway. The snow was falling so hard he could barely see
the outline of her car as it pulled away. Patrick tried to move
into the street to get in line with her rearview mirror, but a
snowbank blocked his way. "Miss Townsend, wait!" he yelled
one last futile time.

He couldn't believe he missed her.

If only he had stayed in his room, like he was supposed
to, he would have been there when she came to visit. It was

like God was punishing him for sneaking out without asking. He buried his face into his mittens and cried, then sat down in the snowbank.

A few moments later, he was being lifted out of the snow. He looked up to find Mrs. Fortini smiling down at him. "C'mon, Patrick," she said. "Let's get you back to your grandfather's." Her black hat and hair were speckled with snow. She pulled him close to her side as they closed the distance. The wind sounded like howling wolves.

Mrs. Fortini was opening his grandfather's vestibule door when suddenly a nice thought came to him, melting his sadness away. Miss Townsend must have come to tell them that his father was almost home. Why else would she have come all the way out here in a snowstorm? If he wasn't home, he must be close. Maybe she came to tell them where to pick him up and when.

❧

Once inside the door, Patrick instantly knew something was wrong. His grandfather seemed upset, not happy. Mrs. Fortini was talking quietly with him, like she didn't want Patrick to hear. She quickly ushered him past his grandfather and took off his winter clothing in the dining room.

"Here, you sit here and I'll get you a nice glass of milk. Are there any cookies left from the plate I brought over?"

Patrick nodded, his eyes still on his grandfather. He was sitting in his favorite chair, slouching badly, as if a single motion would cause him to slide to the floor. His cigar was hanging from his mouth in its usual place, but unlit. His eyes stared straight ahead at some fixed spot on the wall. Beside his ashtray was a bottle of some kind and an empty glass lying on its side.

Patrick turned and watched Mrs. Fortini as she set three

large cookies in front of him and a cold glass of milk. It was so close to dinner, he thought. Why would she want him to eat cookies? She walked back into the living room and stood in front of his grandfather, blocking Patrick's view. Why was his grandfather acting so strangely?

Then it came to him. His grandfather didn't like his dad. That's why he was upset. Patrick's father was coming home, and his grandfather was upset because he didn't want to see him.

Patrick smiled, just a little. He didn't like seeing his grandfather upset, but if it meant his father would be home soon . . . He took a bite of the cookie. They were talking now, arguing quietly about something. Mrs. Fortini was so nice. She was probably scolding him for not being happier about his son coming home from the war. Making sure he didn't do anything to spoil Patrick's surprise.

As Patrick ate the second cookie, he thought he should run right up the stairs and start getting his things together. Should he ask to get up? Should he wait until they were done talking? He couldn't wait another minute. He ran through the living room and scrambled up the stairs.

"Patrick," Mrs. Fortini called. "Where are you going?"

"I'll be right back," he yelled, crossing the hallway into his bedroom. He closed the door so he could be alone. He looked at his parents' picture, thrill rising in his heart. "Mom, I'm not going to be alone much longer. Daddy's almost home. Miss Townsend was just here."

He shifted his gaze to his father's eyes. "I'll be home very soon, son," he imagined him saying, clear as a bell. "You can count on it."

∾

This was terrible. Beyond terrible.

Mrs. Fortini stared at the telegram on the end table; she

could read the words plainly, her vision about the only thing age hadn't captured. Only three words mattered: MISSING IN ACTION. Instantly, she had felt the same heaviness that flooded her soul the day she'd received her news about Frankie.

Poor Shawn, she thought. *God, where is he now? Is he in heaven with you? In a prison camp somewhere?* She looked at the pathetic expression on Collins's face; he looked like a truly tortured man. At least she was able to release her grief, to allow others to share the burden with her. But he was so proud, so self-reliant. His heart had no place to go.

Patrick was safely upstairs. The longer the better, she thought. Somehow, she'd have to get Collins sobered up. She looked at the whiskey bottle. He was barely sober. Her only hope would be to talk him into sleeping it off. Maybe she could bring Patrick home with her for dinner. With this storm, he would have to stay the night.

"Are you through staring at me, Mrs. Fortini?" mumbled Collins. "'Cause if you are, I've got some dinner to make for the boy." He sighed heavily.

"I'm so sorry, Mr. Collins, about the telegram." She was whispering, hoping he'd catch the hint and do the same.

Collins's head turned in the direction of the end table but stopped short of focusing on the telegram. "Thanks. Of all people, I know you understand." A long, awkward pause. "What with your loss, I mean."

"I saw that Miss Townsend leaving just before we came in. Did she have anything to say?"

An angry look instantly grabbed hold of his face. "Nothing of importance."

He began to sit up sloppily. She wondered if he was about to fall forward and took a step back. "Nothing more about Shawn?"

"No," he said curtly. "Could we not talk about her just now?" He stood up and, after a few moments, managed to straighten his posture.

"That's fine," she said in a gentle voice. She was sure a man like Collins would be an angry drunk, best not to stir him. "But how about if you let me fix Patrick dinner? Give you a little time to yourself."

"I can do it," he snapped.

"I know you can. No one is saying you can't—"

"A Collins always does his duty." His glassy focus seemed to look beyond her. "My boy Shawn did his duty, just like a Collins should." He looked down at the bottle then made an effort to find her face again.

It was nice to hear him say something kind about Shawn for a change.

"Look what it got him. Shot down dead by the Nazis."

"Mr. Collins. Don't say that. You don't know that. And please lower your voice. Do you want Patrick to hear?"

"He's got to find out sometime."

"But not this way. You need to get ahold of yourself." He stood there looking at her, as though trying to grasp what she said. "You're right, Shawn did his duty like a good Collins. And right now he needs you to do yours. I know how much you're hurting right now. I've been there, remember? But you've got to put Patrick first. That's what Shawn would have wanted." Oh, why did she say that? Now she was talking as if he were dead. But it seemed to have the right effect.

"Duty. You're right." He even managed a strange sort of smile.

"What are you doing?"

Collins had put his arm around her waist and began to shepherd her toward the door. "You've already got your coat and boots on. Here's your hat. I've got dinner to make. Can't do it standing here talking with you."

"But I offered to—"

"I know, and I appreciate the offer, but I can manage dinner just fine. It'll give me something to do. Take my mind off—" He opened the front door. A burst of icy wind blasted them both. It was still snowing. The storm had picked up in intensity.

Mrs. Fortini realized that once she went outside, there'd be no chance to come back for Patrick. At least not tonight. And if the snow kept up this way, maybe not in the morning either. She stepped back, resisting his arm. "Mr. Collins, I really think you should have some time alone. Let me make Patrick's dinner."

"Nonsense. Look at it out there. He goes to your house, he'd have to stay the night. We'll be fine." He continued to push her toward the door.

She dug in her heels and turned to face him. Wagging her finger in his face, she said, "I'll go, but you've gotta promise me you won't say a word about this telegram to Patrick."

They both stood there as the temperature in the living room quickly began to drop.

"Promise me. You know it's the right thing. If you care at all about Patrick, you've got to keep your grief from harming him. He's already been through too much. I know you didn't care for his mother, but at least try to imagine being a little boy who's just lost his. The only hope he has left is seeing his father come through this door. Don't take that away from him. Not until we know for sure what's happened."

Collins looked down; tears began to form in the corners of his eyes. Mrs. Fortini watched in amazement as he willed them away before they could fall down his cheeks.

"Promise me."

"All right, I promise. Now will you go?"

Twenty-Five

It only took Patrick a few minutes to get his things together. He'd already packed the smaller suitcase and was just about to put his toys in the larger one when he remembered the wooden soldier in the attic. He sat back on the bed, trying to figure out some way to get his grandfather to part with it. There had to be a way, and there was just enough room for it in the bottom corner of the big suitcase. It was just sitting up there in the attic, doing nothing.

Then he got an idea.

Quietly he opened his bedroom door. The hallway was dark, except for a dull light coming up the stairway. He stepped out, listening for any sound. Mrs. Fortini must have gone home, he decided. She would certainly be talking if she were there. He stood still, waiting. Finally, he heard pots clanging in the kitchen, placing his grandfather at a safe distance. He didn't need much time; he knew right where the soldier was.

He tiptoed across the hall and turned the attic doorknob slowly until it clicked. He waited another moment then opened the door and entered the attic stairwell. Fear instantly took hold.

Darkness. Nothing but deep, black darkness. A stairway

leading to nowhere, he thought. Who knew if it still even went to the attic? Anything could be up there, just waiting for a little boy to come up without an adult. Or maybe everything was fine, and he would be perfectly safe. That's the problem with darkness, you never knew until it was too late.

How many times had he and his mother talked about his fear of the dark? It was all his imagination, she'd said. There really wasn't anything to be afraid of. God sees in the darkness, just as easily as the light.

But God wouldn't help him with what he was about to do now.

The switch was just at the top of the stairway, he reminded himself. Just a few more steps to go.

Finally he made it, almost out of breath, and hit the switch. The attic was still there. Everything was the same. He looked to the right, by the soldier's uniform. There it was. He started to hurry but became aware of the sound of his footsteps. He quietly snatched the wooden soldier, then made his way back downstairs after flipping the light switch. He never looked back as he gently closed the door.

Once inside his bedroom, he was glad to find the soldier did fit snugly in the suitcase, just like he thought. This could work. Something like this soldier was meant to be enjoyed, not shoved up in the corner of an old dark attic. Someday when he was older he would finish carving the bottom, maybe even paint it. His dad could help him. He was about to close the lid when he looked up at his parents' picture. He couldn't look at their picture straight on and quickly turned away. He started toward the door but paused as he reached for the knob. He could almost feel his mother's disapproving gaze.

"But it was just sitting up there," he whispered, still facing the door. "He doesn't even care about it. He'd never let me have it; he's way too mean."

"That doesn't matter," she would have said. "And you know it. The point is—it's not yours. It's stealing. You're breaking one of the Ten Commandments."

He turned to face her, his heart sick with disappointment. "But if I ask, he'll never give it to me." He walked over and lifted the suitcase lid. He sighed as he pulled the soldier out, the bayonet catching the corner of his gray sweater. He sat on the edge of the bed, holding it in front of him. He knew what he had to do.

He looked into his mother's eyes, straight on, and said, "I'm sorry."

He walked to the door and opened it quietly. All kinds of sounds were still going on downstairs. He could put it back before his grandfather ever knew what happened. He walked across the dark hallway when a new idea suddenly came to him. He stopped for a moment as it sunk in, then turned toward the stairway.

It could work, he thought. And it wasn't a sin. He'd never know unless he tried.

ᴄᴘᴏ

Collins took another sip of whiskey as he stirred a simmering pot of vegetable soup. He hoped Ida couldn't see him from heaven like this, the looks she'd be giving him. But he needed something to put distance between him and his emotions. He could feel them pressing in, just waiting for a weak moment to burst through again. He had to keep it together. Couldn't let the boy see. Couldn't let the boy know his father was probably dead. *No, stop that,* he thought. *Don't go there. The telegram said missing. Hold on to that. No, don't hold on to that. Don't even think about the whole stinking mess.*

Think about vegetable soup.

He looked at the bottle of whiskey sitting on the counter

to his right, emptier now. He'd brought it in from the living room. He was sure he had another bottle somewhere. Couldn't go out and fetch a new one tonight, not in this storm. He looked back at the pantry, then down at the broken bottle of cooking oil. He'd forgotten to clean up the spill. *Probably going to leave a terrible stain*, he thought, *forever sealing the memory of this night.*

He had known no good would come of bringing a little seven-year-old boy to this house. He had dreaded it the instant he'd said yes to that Townsend woman.

Just doing his duty, he thought.

Look what it got his boy Shawn.

Twenty-Six

Katherine pushed her tiny dinette table two feet closer to the radiator. She was still wearing her gloves and heavy sweater. Not only was her apartment cold, the light wasn't very good, either. She bent down and picked her pen off the floor; it had a nasty habit of rolling off the table due to the sag in the floor. For the last hour, she'd been working on her report, developing the reasons why Patrick should be removed from his grandfather's custody as soon as possible. First thing in the morning she would head into the office and type it up.

Presently, the words were not flowing from her pen. It had been easy to write about Collins's unworthiness to be the parental custodian, to detail his nasty disposition, his inability to offer Patrick any comfort or affection, his total inexperience with small children, and now, add to all that, the telegram and Collins's drunken condition.

The problem was convincing the agency that Patrick should be allowed to live with her.

She looked up from her paper and surveyed the room, imagining what might be said about her accommodations. Her government check afforded her a chilly, one-bedroom, third-floor tenement. Yellowing doilies covered the armrests on the couch and chair hiding the stuffing that stuck out here and there. Her radio didn't work; she hadn't had the time or money to get it repaired. She laughed as she looked at her ridiculous excuse for a Christmas tree standing on a cardboard box in the corner. She had no lights. It was half dead from lack of water. No presents underneath.

Merry Christmas, she thought. *God bless us, everyone.*

They would never approve of her place, any more than they'd approve of her. She was a single woman. *But whatever happened to love?* she thought. *Doesn't love matter?* Her mind began to assemble paragraphs that would express what had been developing in her heart since the moment she'd laid eyes on Patrick.

But instantly she knew such a tack would never work. If anything, her report would have to play down any emotional attachments. She needed logic, not emotion. Somehow she'd have to make Patrick living with her as the most logical choice of all the possible options.

She got up from her chair and grabbed a small blanket from the back of the sofa, wrapped it around her feet, and stared back down at her report.

Logical thoughts were the farthest thing from her mind.

☙

Patrick sat on the top step, clutching the wooden soldier tightly. For the last few minutes, he'd been working up the nerve to ask his grandfather if he could buy it.

That was the new idea, the great master plan.

He had saved over five dollars doing odd jobs back home, like running telephone messages from the grocer to people without phones and shoveling snow from sidewalks. He had been saving to buy his mother a hat for Christmas, one she'd admired every time they walked past Mitchell's Haberdashery.

He quickly shut the memory down before it went any further.

So, five dollars should be more than enough for something somebody just left sitting in their attic. Two dollars was probably enough, but Patrick had decided to offer the entire five. Just to make sure.

There were no longer any sounds coming from the kitchen. His grandfather had been fixing something for dinner judging by the smell. *I better go now*, Patrick thought, *before he starts coming up to call me. If he sees this in my hand before I get to make my offer—*

He hurried down the stairs, rounded the banister, almost tripping over that big box that had been delivered the other day. He'd forgotten all about it. He centered the wooden soldier on the coffee table, then stood blocking its view from the dining room. Waiting.

He reached in his pocket, fingering the dollar bills, just to make sure he could pull them out quickly.

◦∕∕◦

The soup was ready. The table set. He had poured a fresh shot of whiskey for himself, cold milk for the boy. Had only managed to burn himself once on the stew pot. Hardly felt a thing. He was just bringing out the salt and pepper when he noticed a glimmer of light on the floor, reflecting off a spot of cooking oil he must have missed when he'd cleaned up the spill. Better at least get a rag and soak it up, he thought. He'd mop the whole thing in the morning if he wasn't too hung over.

He turned back to the kitchen to get the rag when he saw the boy standing in the living room, as though at attention. "There you are. Saved me the trouble. Just going to yell up for you. You wash your hands?"

Patrick didn't reply.

"Did you wash your hands? You hear me talking to you?"

"I washed them."

"All right, then. Take your seat, and I'll dish out the soup. Watch out for that puddle of oil."

"Okay . . . Grandfather. But there's something I'd like to ask you about first."

Collins stood there, waiting for him to go on. "Well?"

"Remember the other day when I was in the attic?"

Collins nodded, unable to hide the impatience on his face.

"I know my father will be coming home soon. I saw Miss Townsend's car driving away."

Collins felt the next swallow inch down his throat like a jagged rock.

"So that doesn't give me much time. I saw something up there that I kinda want real bad. But I know you didn't want me to play with it just then—"

"What are you going on about?" he asked, the edge returning as he anticipated what was coming next. There was only one thing the boy had been messing with in the attic, as he recalled.

"I've been doing a lot of thinking. My friend Billy said people put stuff in the attic because they can't sell it or don't want to. I'm not sure which one this is, but—"

"Would you just say what you're trying to say, and get it over with?" He took a step in Patrick's direction. Patrick backed up in response, his legs now right up against the coffee table.

"I've got five dollars saved up." He reached in his pocket and pulled out a handful of dollars. Some coins bounced on the rug. One began to roll on its side toward Collins. "I'll get it."

The boy bent over in pursuit. Collins couldn't believe his eyes. Centered on the coffee table behind him was the hand-carved soldier he'd made for Shawn. "You've been back up in the attic," he snapped. "Haven't you?"

Patrick stood up straight. "Yes, sir, I have. But I wanted to—"

Collins's rage needed no help to find its way to the surface. He lunged toward Patrick and grabbed him by the shoulders. "I told you to leave that soldier alone, didn't I?"

"Yes, but—"

"You went up in the attic without even asking permission. At nighttime, no less. And you deliberately took the very thing I told you to never touch again. Didn't you?" Collins was too drunk to see the terror in Patrick's face. "Didn't you!" he screamed.

"But I didn't take it, I was—"

"You didn't take it? Did it walk down here all by itself?"

"That's not what I meant. I . . . I—"

"You don't listen, do you? Got no respect at all, do you? Do whatever you darn well please." He was shaking Patrick with each phrase.

"You're hurting me," Patrick cried.

"Hurting you? I ought to hurt you but good." With that, he tossed Patrick toward the living room. He landed with a thump, half on the throw rug, half on the wooden floor. "Now you put that thing back up there where you found it, you hear? And don't you ever, ever touch it again." His index finger was stabbing the air like a dagger. "And while you're up there, you can just stay up there. No soup for little boys that got no respect."

"Yes, sir," Patrick said through his tears.

Collins waited for one long, tense moment, then said, "Well, go on . . . get!"

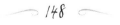

Patrick picked himself off the floor, quickly turning away

from his grandfather's angry glare. Tears were pouring down his face. But these weren't just sad tears; angry tears were mixed in. He didn't want any of his stupid old soup. The only thing he wanted in this house he couldn't have. He hated this place. He hated everything about it. He picked up the wooden soldier and walked toward the stairs.

Out of the corner of his eye, he noticed a piece of paper teetering on the ledge of the end table next to his grandfather's favorite chair, yellow and wrinkled. The only word visible from where he stood was the word "Telegram." He looked up. His grandfather had already gone back in the kitchen.

Maybe it was a telegram about his father. A ray of hope burst through his grief. He tiptoed to the end table and picked it up.

He began to read. At first it was very confusing, but as he read, he felt terrible feelings starting to form inside.

He couldn't understand every word he read.

But he understood enough.

Twenty-Seven

Collins shuffled into the living room, almost tripping over the lip of the throw rug. He had just spent the last thirty minutes sitting at the dining room table, trying to eat the soup he'd made. It had grown cold before he'd finally given up. He'd left the spoon sitting in the bowl, the pot sitting on the stove, a mess sitting on the counter.

He hadn't noticed any of it.

The balance of the whiskey bottle had shaved several degrees from his depression. A soothing numbness had settled over him. He stood at the foot of the stairs, listening for the boy. After several moments of silence, he figured he must have fallen asleep. What nerve, thought Collins. He'd hated sending the boy to bed without supper, but he needed to be taught some respect. It was outright disobedience on the boy's part, almost defiance. He had half a mind to throw out that stupid wooden soldier. Why had he kept it all these years anyway?

Then he remembered the day he had almost thrown it out.

It was the day he'd finally accepted that Shawn and he were through for good. He'd stormed up to his bedroom, grabbed the wooden soldier on the floor beside his dresser, then marched it right past Ida, who was knitting something or another on the sofa.

"Where do you think you're going?" she had said, her voice sharp as steel.

"To be done with this!" Collins yelled, holding up the soldier. "Once and for all."

"Think so? You think throwing that soldier out will punish Shawn somehow?"

"I don't care what Shawn thinks."

"You never did."

"What?"

"You never did care what Shawn thinks. That's half the problem."

"So you're taking his side now?"

"No, I'm just telling the truth. There are no sides to the truth. It's just the way it is. It's not like I haven't seen it all and heard it all for myself. I've been sitting here watching you these last several years. You can't get along with—won't get along with—Shawn, our only son, our only *child*, and now I'm deprived of his company as well."

"What do you want me to do, woman? You've heard the way he's talked to me, the things he's said."

"Yes, I have, and I've heard you too. Which means I've heard both sides . . . quite fully, I might add. And you've never once asked for my observations or advice."

"So what do you want me to do?"

"Do whatever you want to do, Ian. That's all you've ever done. Don't stop now on my account." Then she turned back to her knitting, filling the room and Collins's heart with a guilt so heavy he felt it in his bones.

The guilt of that moment remained alive to this day. It was the reason he had stashed the soldier in the attic instead of the trash. Collins sighed heavily as he sat in his chair. There was no hope now. Shawn was gone. Ida was gone. He had not kept his promise to her, to reconcile with Shawn.

"I am so sorry, Ida. Shawn, I am so sorry." The room was suddenly a blur.

At that moment, his loneliness and despair were complete. They broke through the barriers of the whiskey, and he was overcome by his grief.

He cried like he had never cried before in his life.

∽

It was so cold.

The wind blew right through his coat, scarf, and hat like they weren't even there. The snow trickled into his boots with every step, freezing his feet and toes. And it was still coming down. His arms felt like they were going to fall off carrying this suitcase. Good thing he had decided to bring just the small one. Right now, it was his left arm's turn to drag it behind him in the snow.

He tried not to, but he couldn't stop thinking about the telegram. He knew what "missing in action" meant.

He had suppressed the urge to scream out what he felt after reading those words back in the living room. But he couldn't. Instead, he went up the stairs and cried into his pillow. He couldn't pray. He couldn't think. He couldn't even look at the picture of his mom and dad.

All he knew was he couldn't stay in that house with that old man one minute more.

His father wasn't coming home to get him any day now. The army didn't even know where he was. He realized now that the telegram must have been the real reason Miss Townsend had come to his grandfather's house. In his mind, he had imagined the fight that must have taken place between them. Miss Townsend had driven all that way in the snow to come rescue him, but somehow his grandfather had chased her off. He remembered the card she had given him the first night she had dropped him off, and her words: "*Now, you remember, Patrick, I gave you my card. If you need to call me for any reason, you just call. You don't need your grandfather's permission.*"

That's what his mission was now, to find a telephone.

He couldn't use the one at his grandfather's house; it was in the kitchen, in plain view of his grandfather sitting at the dining room table. He couldn't go to Mrs. Fortini; she might bring him back to his grandfather. He couldn't take that risk. He remembered seeing a telephone at Hodgins's Grocery and was sure he remembered how to get there.

The intersection joining the neighborhood to Clifton Avenue was in sight. If he could just hold out a little longer. He'd call Miss Townsend, and she'd come get him. Tonight he'd be safe and warm with her, with someone who seemed to love him. Her hugs had been the closest to his mom's of anyone he had met.

When he arrived at the end of the street, he leaned against a mailbox on the corner to catch his breath and hide briefly from the wind. He squatted down and buried his face in his coat, hoping to catch a few minutes warmth for his face. His cheeks stung like the dickens, and his jaw felt like it had frozen in place.

The normally busy street had become so quiet, hardly a single car had passed by. He was the only one walking the snow-covered sidewalk. A gust of wind whistled through the mailbox opening, sounding very much like an angry ghost. It startled Patrick, and he quickly got up and moved away.

He looked across the street, trying to spot Hodgins's Grocery through the sheets of blinding snow. But something was wrong. *It's just the snow*, he thought. It was blocking his view to the other side. He didn't see any lights from the many businesses that lined the street. Even the Christmas lights were off. Only the streetlights were lit, and they seemed to blink on and off in the swirling snowfall.

Patrick looked both ways. A lone city bus pulled away from the curb, leaving an empty bench behind. He began his trek across the street, dragging his suitcase as before. As he reached the curb, he realized . . . the lights didn't just *seem* like they were off across the street—they were off! Every business was closed. He sighed and tried to fight back the tears.

What would he do now?

He turned at the sound of the bus driver forcing the gearshift into place and watched as the bus also faded into the darkness.

But this gave him an idea.

He could take a bus downtown, where Miss Townsend worked. He could show her business card to the next bus driver that came along and ask the driver to take him to where she worked. His spirits momentarily lifted, Patrick reached back and picked up his suitcase, making double time to the bus stop bench. He wiped off the several inches of fresh snow and sat down, huddling in the corner, wondering how long he'd have to wait before the next bus came along.

Patrick could not have known that the Philadelphia Transit Authority had, just one hour before, cancelled all remaining routes for that evening due to the fierce snowstorm.

Moments ago, Patrick had witnessed the departure of the last bus of the night.

❧

Back at home, safely snug in a drunken stupor, Collins had moved to his chair after putting on a sweater to ward off the chill. About the only thing the whiskey seemed able to warm was his throat and stomach. He took another drink, deciding to keep a steady flow until it put him to sleep.

The house was quiet at least, the boy upstairs where he belonged. He was not a noisy lad, Collins thought. At least there was that. And he did clean up after himself right well, even better than Shawn did at that age, if he could recall. Shawn. Why did he have to recall Shawn to mind? His eyes fixed on the big cardboard box lying in the corner by the stairway.

There was no reason to restrain his curiosity any longer. The storm would keep Mrs. Fortini and that Townsend woman from stopping by, and the boy was asleep upstairs. He remembered the little cigar box full of Shawn's letters to his wife. A new thought was driving him now, a desperate craving. He wanted to know Shawn again, to know the son he had so completely shut out of his life. His only son.

What had Shawn been like in the years since they parted? What kind of man had he become? What had it been like for him over there, up until the end? Collins had to know. The letters could help him find out.

He stumbled as he got out of his chair, but he didn't care. He crawled to the big box and opened it quickly. He lifted the shoe box carefully from its hold and carried it back to his chair.

"Shawn," he said aloud, staring at the box. "I have missed you so much." He lifted the lid and untied the shoestring holding the letters together. "We used to be so close," he muttered. "I've been such an old fool."

After thumbing through a handful, it was obvious they had been sorted by date, the oldest at the top of the stack. Each letter was a single page, folded in thirds. Collins noticed the word "V-Mail" printed at the bottom and remembered reading something about this in the newspaper. In order to conserve cargo space, the military microfilmed the GIs' original letters, then reduced them in size before reprinting them. Centered at the heading of each letter was a square with Shawn's Philadelphia address on Clark Street.

There must've been at least fifty of them. He couldn't read them all, but perhaps he could read at least five or ten tonight, a small sampling from front to back. He took a deep breath and tried to steady his trembling hand as he unfolded the first letter and began to read.

January 28, 1943

My darling Liz,

I try to fling myself into whatever I'm doing, try not to think about how much I miss you and Patrick, but nothing works. I did get the picture you sent. I'm guarding it with my life. Is it possible you've grown even more beautiful in the four months we've been apart?

We'll be heading to England soon. That's as much detail as I can say. You can send future letters to me using the same address and they'll forward them to me until I get a new one. I don't know exactly where I'll be going. We've been told to say to our families "somewhere in England."

I did so well in my flight training, they're promoting me to pilot. I really enjoy flying, seems to come naturally to me. We'll see how I do in the real world. Needless to say, keep the prayers flowing.

Tell Patrick I loved his letter. I can't believe how well he's writing. I understood every word. He's my little man. There's this little boy I see in town sometimes. Every time I see him, I think of Patrick. I know I'm doing the right thing being here, but it is so hard trying to get along without you both.

I love you so much,
Shawn

P.S. I wrote a separate letter to the landlord, pleading with him to be patriotic and get off your back about the rent. I told him the money is on the way. Let me know if he gives you any more trouble.

∎

March 14, 1943

My beautiful wife,

This is the hardest letter I've had to write so far. Do you see the date? I'm trying to imagine where you are right now as I write this. The way you've set your hair, what dress you're wearing, what perfume. I know you like to think more of the anniversary of our first date. But this is the date I have to start with, the day I first laid eyes on you, sitting there across the Carnegie library from me.

I think I knew I loved you right then. Everything else from that point just intensified that first awareness. There must have been a thousand pretty girls at that college, at least that's what I'm told. The moment I saw you, they all faded away. I don't know where I would be if you hadn't finally returned my affections.

Even now with my life so uncertain, the realities

of war confronting me on all sides, I only need to think back to that first moment, and what came after, to be carried away into bliss. I don't mind that you put me off for so long, that you held out until I came to the same faith. Your convictions became part of my deep, abiding attraction.

Now it is only God's love that sustains me on a day like today, when we must be apart. Give our little man a big hug for me. Tell him I think of him many times a day. As always, only the passing of days is needed for my love for you to grow.

I love you,
Shawn

■

May 5, 1943

My darling Liz,

Just read your latest stack of letters. Tell Patrick the drawings he sent are wonderful. Especially like the one where he and I are playing catch out front of our apartment (at least I think that's what it is, better ask him first). I guess I don't mind you working part-time while Patrick's in school. I prefer that to asking my father for help. When I get my next promotion, it should be enough, or at least make it so things won't be so tight for you. Battlefield promotions happen a lot in wartime. So it shouldn't be long before I can send you a bit more.

Hopefully you can find a job working around a lot of old ladies (that would be ideal), so none *of those 4Fs give you a hard time. You know they will, the way you look. It's not your fault. I know you don't flirt. You can't help it if you're stuck being beautiful. But really, I do trust you, and that's a major load off my mind. Almost every week or so a guy over here gets a "Dear John" letter from some gal back home, saying how sorry she is but she's just too lonely to wait anymore. Makes me so mad. It devastates these guys. What are these girls thinking? We're over here on a vacation? Happened to one of my crew a month ago, Tommy Hastings. He's still not over it. Ran out of space, sorry.*

Thanks for your timeless love and devotion.

You know you have mine . . . always,
Shawn

"I prefer that to asking my father for help."

Ian Collins read this line over several times in his head, then set the letter aside. Up until now he'd been drawn into Shawn's letters with genuine interest, even a growing sympathy. He didn't think he'd show up anywhere in the letters, and was offended by the one place so far that he did. Apparently, Shawn's wife had asked Shawn in an earlier letter to consider asking him for financial help.

Collins didn't know how he would have responded if she had asked. But that wasn't the point. He had a mattress full of money, money stashed all around the house, and big heaping bagfuls of it down at the bank. And here things were tight for Shawn's wife and child and Shawn forbids them from even asking him for help.

Collins lifted his head and worked out the kink in his neck. How many letters had he read? The room started coming back into focus. He heard the wind whipping up outside, a banging sound against the porch. That big maple tree branch; he knew he should have had that thing cut down. He listened for a moment for the boy. Didn't sound like it woke him up.

Then he remembered how he'd spoken to him earlier. He should have kept his tongue. It was just the strong drink talking, or else the depression about Shawn's plane going down. He looked over at the Western Union telegram. *My poor boy*, he thought. *Where are you now? Are you with your mother and the angels?*

He took another drink. As it warmed his insides, he decided he had to read on. He realized even worse things might be said, but he had to know. These letters may be the only link that remained between him and Shawn.

For Ida's sake, if not for his own, he had to read on.

May 24, 1943

Dear Liz,

Saw the sun for the first time yesterday in I don't know how many months. I just wanted to sit there in my chair by the airfield and let it beat on my face. I blocked out the noise all around me, and it was like I was there with you at the shore. Remember the summer before last at Wildwood? For a few minutes we were together on the beach again, holding hands, eyes closed, listening to the waves brush against the beach, Patrick building a little castle around my feet.

My dream ended when a mechanic working on my plane dropped a monkey wrench, almost hitting me in the head. I opened my eyes, and there I was, so very far away from both of you. But for a moment, we were near.

So much is happening around here, most I can't talk about (loose lips sink ships, etc.). But I am trying to keep a decent journal, so that when I'm home you can get a clearer picture. Let's see if the censors let me say this much (if the next few sentences are not blacked out, you'll know). On yesterday's mission it was the strangest thing. No flak or enemy fighters the entire time, all the way there and back. After a while, I felt like an airline pilot taking a nice ride across the European countryside. Perhaps one day I can bring you back when this is all over and do just that. Take you and Patrick for a scenic flight over Europe. Breakfast in London, dinner in Paris.

All my love,
Shawn

■

June 3, 1943

Dear Liz,

Just finished reading your latest batch of letters. Everything was going great till I got to the last one. I'm sure you know the one I mean. Maybe it's just coming at a bad time (had a rough week). I know you're only trying to help, as you have so often in this issue. As my wife, you have a right to inquire. And I'm not questioning your motives. I'm just not sure I'm ready to take the step you're suggesting.

In my heart, I think he has to be the one to make the first move. I've always had to be the one to do it. All my life. It was right growing

*up, when I was under his roof, but he had no
right to treat me, treat us, the way he did after
we got together and certainly not after we got
married. I haven't even told you all the things he
said. Years don't change what is right and what is
wrong. I feel if I'm made to give in now, he will
never change, and it will establish a precedent in
our relationship that will never be undone. There's
a difference between showing honor and coming
under someone's control.*

*I'm sorry to go against your wishes on this,
love. Your heart is clearly more merciful than
mine. But I'm afraid I'm going to have to say no
at this time. If he contacts you, and you sense
there's been a heart change of even the smallest
degree, you have my standing permission to respond.
But, please, don't initiate anything from your end.
At least not now. I'm sorry.*

*All my love,
Shawn*

Collins set the letter down. Obviously, Shawn was referring
to him in the letter. How could it be about anyone else? He
read it through again, then once more. His anger percolat-
ing, seeking permission to ascend, but he kept it at bay. He
wasn't even sure why.

Then he realized.

He knew of Shawn's stubbornness; like Ida always said,
the apple doesn't fall far from the tree. But something he
had always been certain of, had always counted on, had just
dissolved in a moment. He wasn't sure what should fill the
hole left in its wake. He had always believed Shawn's wife
had been behind the conflict between them, the root cause of
him pulling away. She had used her beauty to lure him from

their world into her own. And Collins was sure she had been the reason why Shawn hadn't even attempted to apologize all these years.

Had he been wrong about Elizabeth all this time?

Elizabeth.

He realized he had never even said her name before. She was always "that woman." But that woman had apparently been trying to talk his son into reconciling with him, not trying to keep them apart.

Maybe she had never been.

His anger released its tension in a sigh. He lifted his head back, drew in a deep breath, and continued to read.

July 29, 1943

My lovely Liz,

Had a strange thing happen earlier today, got a sense of what it must be like for our ground crews every time we get sent out on a mission.

Our plane was getting some repairs, so we couldn't take off with our bomb group today. I went out to the airfield just the same to watch everyone take off. After the last plane flew out of sight, all the ground crews just stood there, dozens of them, staring off into the sky for several minutes. Then one by one, they made their way back to the barracks. I hung around the base a few hours until word spread the bombers were returning. You should have seen the crews running to the edge of the airfield, straining to get a glimpse. Different ones would yell out and cheer as their particular plane came into view and touched down.

Then you saw the crews waiting for the planes that didn't come back, the grief and heartache on

their faces, as they tried to console each other
that there still might be hope (the hope that they
might at least be POWs). Never realized how hard
it was on them until today.

How hard it must be on you, my darling, when
waiting is all you can do.

All my love,
Shawn

Collins set the letter down, reflecting on the last paragraph in particular.

It dawned on him . . . he had not been waiting for Shawn.

His only son had been living in harm's way, valiantly fighting for his country for well over a year. But Collins had not been home pining away about Shawn's safety. Other families had. All over town. Fathers, mothers, brothers, sisters, and cousins. It was all they talked about. *How's your boy doing? Have you heard from him lately? What's the latest from the front? I'm sure he'll be okay.*

Collins had dismissed it as so much idle chatter. Street noise, like the rumbling of car engines or the screeching of trolley cars. It was as if he had no stake in this war. As if he had no son.

No son . . . and now that might just be the case. No wife, and now . . . no son.

In his mind he saw a small group of unnamed mechanics in England, staring at the edge of a runway, staring off toward the horizon, longing for a glimpse of Shawn's plane at the end of that last mission. He felt, for the first time, what they must have felt when all the planes had returned safely home that day. All except one.

Shawn's plane.

Collins and this crew shared the same grief. Only Collins's grief was but a few hours old.

And already it was becoming unbearable.

Tears began to roll down his cheeks again. What was he doing? Why put himself through this torture? He wiped his face on his sleeve and forced the tears to stop.

Then a new disturbing thought came . . . if Shawn's plane never came home, would there ever be a body sent home to bury?

Did Shawn's body still exist? Had it disintegrated in some terrible fireball in the sky? Was it lying in some cornfield, twisted and mangled in some wreckage? How does one grieve properly without a proper funeral?

All Collins had to show for his son's life was this telegram . . . and these letters.

But that wasn't all.

There was the boy. Patrick. He said his name aloud. "Patrick."

He looked up the stairwell. He thought about going upstairs, just to look in on him. Maybe he could whisper in his ear how sorry he was for treating him so badly. Tell him what he really thought of him: that he was a fine lad, with good manners, hardworking, handsome. The boy—Patrick—shouldn't be made to pay for the falling-out he'd had with his father. It wasn't his fault. And he was all the family Collins had left now.

All that was left of Shawn.

He looked down at the cigar box sitting on the coffee table. He couldn't just walk upstairs now, not unless it was the last time for the night; he'd never make it back down. And what if Patrick woke up before he did in the morning, came down to find this mess?

No, a few more letters and he'd have sampled the entire stack. Painful as it was, he decided he had to read at least a few more. Then he'd put things back where they belonged and head up the stairs.

September 6, 1943

My darling Liz,

Sorry to hear you lost your job at the bakery. But I have good news, I've been promoted to captain, which brings a decent pay raise. Should cover whatever money you've lost. I'll let you decide if you need to find other work after you get my next check. I know you'll do what's best. I'm so proud of the way you've been handling things while I'm gone.

I've noticed something in your last batch of letters, hinting at wanting to take Patrick to see my father (I think that's where the hints are going). You know how I feel about this, but I can see you have no intention of dropping the idea altogether. So let's stop hinting. Go ahead and write me a letter explaining exactly what you're thinking. Being around life and death issues on a regular basis has a way of softening the heart.

So much going on here, wish I could speak freely. Twelve more missions and that day will finally come. That means I'm past the halfway mark of 25. Then you'll be in my arms again, my love. Just imagine. I do . . . all the time.

All my love,
Shawn

■

Oct. 3, 1943

My darling,

Finally got your batch of letters (we wondered

if the mail ship got sunk). You can't imagine how precious they are to me. I hold each one like thousand dollar bills. When they come, I drop everything until I read them, or if the army delays me, I think of nothing else until I get back to them. I can think of no sadder sight on this earth than a soldier left standing empty-handed after mail call is through.

Had an interesting thing happen on my last mission. The plane directly to our left carried one of those newsreel photographers taking movies of our flight. He definitely got an eyeful (got pounced twice by German fighters and the flak was so thick you could walk on it). The thing is, I'm sure my plane will be in that footage. How can it not be, we were right next to him? So be on the lookout at the theaters a few weeks from now. Tell Patrick if he sees a bunch of B-17s in the air to be looking for my plane, "Mama's Kitchen." Tell him that's his daddy flying that thing. I miss you both so much.

All my love,
Shawn

■

November 18, 1943

Dear Liz,

Sorry about ignoring your letter about my dad. You're right, I did get it, read it several times, in fact. But I just wasn't ready to respond. Here I'd given you the green light to make your case, then I chickened out. I am facing mortal danger in enemy skies on a regular basis, and I'm afraid to face my own heart and where it may lead on this thing.

Well, your last appeal did get through. I've never thought about forgiveness quite that way before. That it's a command from Christ, not a suggestion. And that my motivation needs to be the forgiveness I have received, not that the other party deserves it. I don't deserve the mercy God has shown me, either. I guess I had been holding out, waiting for my dad to make the first move, and feeling justified until he did. But I know that day may never come, and I'm keeping Patrick from ever knowing his own grandfather because of my stubborn pride. I've asked God to forgive me, and now I'm asking you. One day, by God's grace, I hope to be able to do the same with him. You have my permission to make contact with him. Have no idea what he'll do or say, but I'll pray.

Love you so much,
Shawn

Collins set the letter down and sat back, shaking his head in quiet resignation to a reality he could no longer ignore. He had been all wrong about Shawn's wife Elizabeth, totally wrong. The evidence was clear. She had been trying to bring him and Shawn together, not keep them apart. And now—with this letter—it was clear she had finally broken through.

Collins noticed that he was finally near the bottom of the stack, only a couple more left to go. He looked again at the date of this last letter: "Nov. 18, 1943." Just over a month ago, only four weeks before the car accident that took Elizabeth's life. A sweeping sadness engulfed him now. Elizabeth never knew she had so little time left. And she had gone so early in life. At least he and Ida had shared a life together, an entire life. But then a sadder thought . . . at least for Collins. Shawn and his wife Elizabeth were already reunited.

Collins was the one left alone.

The tears started flowing once more. But he forced himself to read on; he was so near the end.

Just two more letters.

November 22, 1943

Dear Liz,

I am so cold as I write this. My hand is literally trembling. I write a little, breathe on my knuckles, write a little more. Remember how I used to be the one to keep you warm? You'd stick your freezing hands under my sweater—I'd jump at the shock? Couldn't help you now.

Another Thanksgiving apart. What will you and Patrick be doing, I wonder. I still remember last year . . . the smell of turkey throughout the apartment, your wonderful mashed potatoes, the stuffing and green beans, all smothered in gravy, Christmas music on the radio. Why do I torment myself this way? I'm facing a mess hall full of guys, none of whom wants to be here, standing in line as some guy slaps down a pile of Thanksgiving food, all flung together in a mush.

I am praying this will be our last Thanksgiving apart. It could be. It's what I live for—seeing you again, holding you in my arms. Tell Patrick how proud I am of him for taking such good care of you.

All my love,
Shawn

■

December 6, 1943

My Darling Liz,

Thank you so much for sending that new picture of you and Patrick. My heart skipped a beat when it fell out of the envelope. You don't know how precious it is to get a fresh glimpse of your face again. Could you even be more beautiful than before? And Patrick, he looks like he's grown 2 or 3 inches, standing there next to you.

John Talbot, a new pilot bunking with us, was looking over my shoulder and said, "Is THAT your wife?" He had that same dazed look so many men would get when we'd walk around together (and it was all I could do to keep myself from decking them). But I just said, "Can you believe I have this waiting for me back home?" How did I ever wind up with you? You are so out of my league.

I've included twenty-two dollars with this letter. Buy yourself and Patrick something nice for Christmas (I got it from a wealthy English gentleman, after I stopped to change his flat tire . . . wouldn't take no for an answer). It must be meant for you.

Merry Christmas and all my love,
Shawn

P.S. Looking forward to hearing all about your big adventure with my father.

Collins gently laid the last letter back in the shoe box and sat up straight.

The date on it was December 6; Shawn had written it just a few weeks ago. And considering how long it took military mail to reach home, Elizabeth must have read this just a day or two before the car accident that ended her life. She would not be waiting for Shawn when he got home, and Shawn would not be coming home. She was gone; now Shawn was gone. His Ida, gone. And here he was in this chair, this room, this house, the least worthy of them all to be spared.

What purpose could God have in that?

His head turned slowly toward the bottle of whiskey. He reached for it with an unsteady hand, determined not to drink from the bottle. He set it in front of him, then reached for the shot glass sitting on its side. But he knocked it over trying to right it, and it slammed to the floor. It didn't shatter but made such a noise that it startled him.

After a few hushed minutes, it became clear Patrick had not been aroused. Collins released the pent-up air in his lungs and carefully poured. He had to keep the mouth of the bottle several inches away from the glass, to keep them from clinking together, his hand was shaking so. The whiskey went down in a single shot, and it warmed his insides, the only warmth he felt.

All his comfortable routines had been shattered the day Patrick arrived, but now he realized it was not only his present life that had been overturned, but his past and his future as well. His memories, just moments ago arrayed like statues on a well-manicured lawn, were now broken in pieces. Not a single one intact. He'd had it all wrong from the beginning.

About everything.

Elizabeth did not hate him, though now for the life of him he could not understand why. She had not tried to keep Shawn away, probably never had. She had been trying to push them back together, just like Ida would have wanted. And she succeeded, at least in part. Shawn had given her permission to visit. That had to be the "big adventure" Shawn spoke of in the "P.S." of this last letter. Elizabeth was planning to visit him, and to bring Patrick.

His heart sank as he thought on it. He knew how he'd have responded. His hatred and prejudice would have been right there at the surface. And he'd likely not have kept a civil tongue, maybe even run them both off with a broom or a stick. And Ida would have been watching from heaven, and so would God. And Collins might have put his mortal soul in peril by the whole exchange.

Tears started to fall again from his face, directly onto the table, his head bowed so low. What a waste of a man he had become. What a total waste of a man.

"Elizabeth," he said aloud. "Was a mercy you never got your chance to visit. I'd have ruined it for us all."

✍

After composing himself a bit, he decided to put things back the way they were and head up to bed. He wasn't sure he could sleep but was exhausted enough to try. He put the letters back in the shoe box exactly as he'd found them. But really, who was left to know any better?

He started to slide the box back into the corner when his eyes fell on the telegram. He picked it up, trying to decide what to do with it. Better in the box, he thought, than lying around in the open for Patrick to find.

He reopened the box and was just about to put the telegram in when two other papers caught his eye. They were wedged up against the side of the box beside a hairbrush, folded in thirds. Collins lifted them out and noticed they were larger than Shawn's letters but looked to be letters for sure, on two different kinds of stationery.

He sat back on the chair, holding them both, and picked one to read and set the other on his lap. As soon as he unfolded the pages, his hands began to tremble.

It was Ida's handwriting.

A bit shaky, the way she wrote near the end, but it was unmistakably her writing. At the top of the letter, he was startled as he read the words "Dear Elizabeth."

It was a letter from Ida to Shawn's wife.

Dear Elizabeth,

Thank you so much for your visits of late. I'm sorry we have to be so sneaky, but I couldn't take the chance that Ian would find out. He's just not ready for something like that, but I know my time is short, and I can't wait around for his heart to change. I know God understands and will forgive me going against his wishes.

How I hoped I could see Patrick in person, but the hospital won't allow it. But I cherish the picture you brought of him. I look at it often. You can't imagine how much like Shawn he looks. I have asked one of the nurses a favor, and she assures me she will oblige. When my time comes, I explained this picture must be returned to you without Ian's knowledge. He'll have enough to worry about without trying to handle this (that we've been visiting).

There is only one prayer I pray every day, that God would reveal himself to my husband before he dies, and that my husband would come to know him the way I have these past few months. I know that would be enough to melt his cold heart and restore his relationship with you all.

I have you to thank, Elizabeth, for the change in

my heart. Before you shared the gospel with me, I must admit, though I've believed in God all these years, I dreaded the thought of my final hour and what fate might await me. Ian always said I'd go straight to heaven, but he's only judging the outside. God knows the sins of my heart, and I was sure great suffering awaited me the moment this illness took its final stroke.

But I did as you said and began to read the Bible, starting with the Gospels. I had never read the Bible in all my life.

But I saw my Savior as I read, unfolding within the pages, and marveled at his words and deeds. And it has changed me completely. Jesus is so real to me now, and now I can't wait to see him face-to-face. I read the verses in Paul's epistles that you gave me and, combined with the Gospels, I now understand what you meant about Jesus dying for my sins on the cross, once for all. Something happened in my heart as I read, and I knew it was all true.

Then for the first time, maybe in my life, I talked to Jesus without formal words or recited prayers. And a peace and joy came over me like I've never known. Right then, I knew I had no reason to fear my death. I lay here now, my body racked with pain, life ebbing away, and totally unconcerned about it all. All I know is joy and serenity.

The only thing on earth that troubles me is the brokenness in my family. But I have prayed and asked God to please sort it all out after I'm gone, and I have peace that he will.

I feel inside I don't have many days left, but please know, because of you these days will be spent so much better. You keep praying too, and I

*know one day God will do something to make a way
for our family to be whole again.*

*With much love,
Ida*

Collins was stunned.

He read the letter again, slowly. By the end of the second
reading, he felt totally sober. But he was so conflicted inside.
Just reading something Ida had written that he'd never seen,
pages that her hands had handled, warmed his heart and
beckoned fond memories. But realizing the letter told of a
secret betrayal and a total disregard for his wishes aroused
his anger. Yet he knew Ida did these things only because he
had been so stubborn—when it was now clear Elizabeth was
not the enemy he'd made her out to be.

He felt more ashamed than angry.

The ache inside was painful and wholly unfamiliar. He
looked around the room, as though some path might open
up to him, a place he could run to and hide from the pain. He
looked down at the second letter. Clearly not written by Ida.
He let Ida's letter fall to the table and picked up the other.
He read the first few words, just the date and the greeting.
It took a few moments for their significance to sink in. He
read them again.

"Oh no," he said aloud.

He read the greeting and especially the date again. But
what else could it be? There were two pages. He quickly
flipped to the second page to read the ending, and his fears
were confirmed.

It said: "With all my love, Liz."

It was a letter addressed to Shawn and written by Elizabeth
. . . on the very day she died.

Shawn had never seen it. No one ever had, for it had never been sent.

Dec. 18, 1943

My dearest Shawn,

Your last letter was so wonderful. You can't imagine what it does to my day when the mail includes something from you. Every day I quickly rummage through whatever comes in, looking for only one thing. And when it comes . . . to know I'm holding something you wrote just for me. Something your fingers have touched.

Well, today is the big day. With your blessing now, I'm going to ride across town and pop in on your father for a visit. I don't mind saying, I couldn't be more nervous about this. I know you've told me not to get my hopes up, but I can't help it. Something has got to give on this thing, and I know it grieves God that our family is so torn apart. I'm willing to do whatever it takes to make an end to all this strife.

Perhaps today will just be a beginning. I'm not expecting your father to throw his arms around me and give me a big kiss on the cheek. In fact, I'm bringing Patrick with me but not telling him where we're going, just in case it doesn't go well. I'll leave him in the car until I see how your father responds. Hopefully, he'll at least invite us in, and I can begin to chip away at the dividing wall between us. But I don't think I'm going to be the primary instrument of peace.

I don't know how, but when I pray, I get the sense that Patrick is going to factor in on this somehow. He looks so much like you and yet he is so innocent (not that you are so guilty . . . you know what I mean).

Wouldn't it be an amazing thing, though, if by this Christmas this long-standing feud would finally be over? That for the first time in Patrick's young life he'd actually get a present from his grandfather? It doesn't have to be a big one, just anything. And then 1944 would usher in a new beginning. The war would end, and you'd come home, and we'd all be together again.

I can just see your face as you read this, scrunching up in disbelief at my naïveté and optimism. Then you'd break into a smile as a glimmer of hope broke through that what I said could possibly come true (and then that smile would quickly return to a frown as you thought of the right words to say that would balance me out).

Well, don't balance me out this time, my love. Hope with me. I don't know what God is going to do, but I'm confident his wisdom and power will make a way. He is famous for "making roadways in the wilderness, and rivers in the desert."

I know we're called to overcome evil with good. So, I'm going armed with a mincemeat pie (which I abhor), because you said it was his favorite (I'm trusting you on this). And I'm wearing my green dress and hat, even though I'm not Irish. I know this is what your mom wanted too, so that gives me strength. She told me herself just before she died. I promised her, if it took the rest of my life, I wouldn't stop trying to bring us all back together again.

I'm holding on to this letter until tomorrow, so I can include with it another letter after the visit, *to let you know how things went. So there should be two letters in this envelope.*

And there will be something else in the envelope, not so easily seen but always present . . .

That is, my unending love,
Liz

It was too amazing to believe. Collins looked at the date again and considered everything the letter said. It had to be true.

Elizabeth was on her way to see him the day she died. With Patrick.

Collins tried to remember what little information he'd been told by Miss Townsend about the accident. It happened just two miles from where she lived, so he'd never even considered the possibility before. Elizabeth was riding through a busy intersection when some guy in a stolen car happened to be fleeing the police. He ran a red light and slammed right into her car door. It put him in the hospital with some broken bones, but Elizabeth was killed instantly. The miracle in the whole thing was Patrick, although knocked unconscious, was otherwise unharmed. Fortunately, he couldn't recall a thing.

But the pieces of the puzzle were coming together now, and how he wished they were not. If Elizabeth hadn't been trying so hard to reunite the family, she would not have been in the car that day, at least not heading in that direction. The juvenile fleeing the police would have missed her completely or else hit somebody else. She'd be alive, and Patrick would have a mom. And Shawn would have a—

Or would he? Would Shawn even be coming home?

This whole thing was becoming such a nightmare. Now Patrick had no one, he thought. No one but him. And look how he'd been treating his only grandson, not just recently but for his entire life. And how he had treated the boy's father, his own son Shawn.

And Elizabeth.

Even Ida.

He had kept Ida from spending any time with her only son and grandson, even on her deathbed. For no reason except his stubborn pride.

He was the source behind all the heartache and confusion for everyone. Shawn had married, what seemed like now, a fine woman. And Collins had never given her a chance. He had more money than he could spend in two lifetimes, and here they were, barely able to make ends meet. Collins didn't even know about their situation. Why? Because he'd cast them all into exile. So he could live all alone in this cold, dreary house, squandering his remaining years in isolation and solitude. Then Elizabeth dies, his only grandson is brought to him, and all he thinks about is . . . when is he going to leave.

What kind of punishment would a man like this face before God?

There could be no easy penance for him. Collins would be headed straight for hell.

"God forgive me," he cried. "But I do deserve hell and more. What can I do to make this right? Can I even make it right?"

Twenty-Eight

Collins walked about downstairs, starting to close up the house. It was only a little before 8:00 p.m., but he was totally spent. His mind had mercifully gone numb, more from the day's events than the whiskey. He was so glad that the boy—*Patrick . . . his name is Patrick*—stayed asleep the entire time he'd been reading the letters.

Before ascending the stairway, he took one last glance around the room to make sure everything was in place. The last thing he saw was the big box from Elizabeth's apartment. How it had grown in value over the last few hours.

He climbed the stairs, thinking about what a fine boy Patrick really was, now that he could think more clearly. Collins knew Patrick didn't shovel his driveway to get that wooden soldier. He did it for love, or maybe to get Collins to stop treating him so poorly. But he wasn't some scheming conniver, just a little boy who'd lost his mother and was thrust out into the world all alone. Even in Collins's house, he realized . . . Patrick must still feel all alone.

But tomorrow that changes, Collins thought. *Tomorrow we will start over. And I will treat him the way he should be treated.*

He didn't even know where to begin, but he knew he must try. "Ida," he whispered aloud as he reached the final step, "I'm going to do this. I'm finally going to do what you've wanted me to do all along."

He turned on the hall light and glanced toward Patrick's room. Part of him wanted to just rush in and scoop Patrick up in his arms, just to say something kind or encouraging. He headed there but stopped. *Let the boy sleep*, he thought. *He's had a horrible day. We'll start fresh in the morning.* He walked to his own room and got dressed for bed.

A few minutes later he went into the bathroom and turned on the light. As he reached for his toothbrush, he looked toward Patrick's room. Something caught his eye, something seemed off. He noticed a suitcase on the floor, next to the bed. It belonged in the closet, had been there since Patrick arrived. He walked over to have a look. The suitcase was open and things were spilled out across the floor. He turned on the light.

"Oh no." The bed was empty, still made up from this morning. Patrick was gone.

"Patrick!" he yelled. "Patrick? Where are you, son?" He ran toward the attic steps. "Please let him be there." His heart sank as he opened the door. The stairs went upward into solid darkness. Still Collins scrambled up, yelling Patrick's name all the while.

But there was no reply. Where could he be?

He rushed downstairs, faster than he'd moved in years. Maybe Patrick was in the basement. He had no reason to think he'd be there, but where else could he be? But once again, as he opened the basement door, it was totally black. Still Collins went down, calling out Patrick's name.

Still no reply.

He went back up and turned on a lamp in the living room.

That's when he noticed Patrick's coat and boots were gone. It made no sense. How could Patrick have gone outside? Collins had been in the living room reading the letters for hours. When could he have gone, where could he have gone?

"Mrs. Fortini." He breathed a loud sigh. *That's it. Patrick must have gone next door.* He had either gotten mad or afraid at the way Collins treated him earlier and ran next door. Without thinking, Collins opened the front door and was instantly stung by the chill rushing in from the vestibule. He'd completely forgotten about the snowstorm. It was coming down in sheets, almost sideways, driven by a howling wind. Still he went out, straining to see any signs of life next door.

Good, he thought. Through the white haze he could see lights on in Mrs. Fortini's living room. *That's where Patrick must be. He's probably sitting in her living room right now, eating cookies and listening to Christmas songs on the radio.* He stepped back inside the house, shivering as he closed the door.

But why hadn't she called?

Mrs. Fortini wouldn't have let Patrick stay over there this long without calling. Then he remembered . . . he wasn't in his present state of mind when they parted. He was depressed and angry, fueled by whiskey and hate. He couldn't recall her final words, but she was plenty sore at him when she left. She probably decided Patrick was better off at her place tonight, planned to square things up with him in the morning.

But it still didn't sit right with him, didn't seem the way Mrs. Fortini would operate.

He walked over to the hutch, picked up a white card next to the telephone, and dialed the middle of three numbers written down. He steadied himself, took a deep breath, and waited.

"Hello?"

What should he say? How should he—

"Hello? Is anyone there?" she was yelling. He smiled. Mrs. Fortini, being Italian, always yelled whenever she talked on the phone.

"Mrs. Fortini? This is Ian from next door."

"Ian? Is that you? Is everything all right?"

"I'm fine." He tried to soften his tone. "I'm just calling to find out if—"

"Is Patrick all right? Is he hurt? Is anything wrong?"

Collins heart fell. Then the room began to spin. He clutched the edge of the hutch.

"Ian . . . Mr. Collins, what's wrong, what's the matter?"

He was not with her. *Oh God, no.*

"Ian, talk to me . . . what's wrong?"

"It's Patrick . . . I don't know. He's gone."

"What?"

"He's gone. I thought he must be with you."

"What do you mean, gone?"

"He's not in his room, he's nowhere in the house."

"Did you check the attic?"

"I checked everywhere. He's gone. I don't know what—"

"Ian, he can't be gone. There's a blizzard outside. Where could he go?"

"I don't know!" he yelled. "But he's gone. What have I done? Patrick . . ."

"Ian, Ian, get hold of yourself. You've got to call the police. You need to hang up the phone right now and call the police."

"I've got to go; I've got to find him."

"No . . . listen to me, wherever he is, we need to get some help. You can't just go out there like this. It's freezing outside, and this storm is supposed to get even worse. We're just two old people, Ian. We need help. And we've got to act now. If Patrick's out there in this and we don't find him soon, he'll freeze to death."

Collins dropped to the floor. He just sat down like a child, propping himself up with one hand, holding his head with the other. "I don't know what to do," he cried. "God, please, don't do this to me. Don't let me lose Patrick, not now."

༈

"Ian . . . are you there? Ian?" Mrs. Fortini waited on the line a few moments more. "Ian," she yelled, then waited again. "Are you there?" She hung up the phone. What happened to him? Did he have a heart attack? She couldn't wait any longer.

She dialed the operator. "Operator, this is an emergency, get me the police."

"One moment, ma'am."

A few moments later, someone from the closest precinct was on the phone. She did her best to describe the situation, trying to contain her fears. The officer on call didn't seem to grasp the seriousness of the situation. All he talked about was the storm and how the storm made it impossible for anyone to help them now. The snowplows weren't expected to be out till the morning, and even then it would take hours, if not days, to reach individual neighborhoods.

"Sir," she finally said, "there's a little seven-year-old boy lost out in this storm. His mother just died a few weeks ago, and we just got a telegram today saying his father is missing in action. For all I know, his grandfather just had a heart attack next door. Can't you do anything? You're the police! Who else can we call?"

"Okay, okay. Let me get your number, and I'll see what I can do."

She gave him her number, then Collins's too. "I'm going next door to see what happened. Try my number first, then his."

She hung up the phone, put on her big coat and boots, and made her way toward the door. Just before she left, she reached in her coat pocket and made sure she still had the card Katherine Townsend had given her the other day at Hodgins's Grocery.

Twenty-Nine

"What do you mean, gone?" Katherine Townsend felt her legs go weak. She began to sit, barely connecting with a nearby dinette chair. On the other end of the phone, Mrs. Fortini was still talking, saying other things about Patrick, but the words stopped penetrating. Katherine was supposed to be good at dealing with family tragedies—she'd been doing it for years—but she had no resources to draw from for this. And she knew why. Patrick mattered. He mattered from the first hour she'd spent with him that first day at the apartment on Clark Street. He mattered more to her than any child she'd ever worked with, any child she had ever known.

"I am so afraid for him," said Mrs. Fortini. "We don't know how long he's been out in this weather, and I can't get the police to take me seriously. They say the storm's too bad for them to do anything. I don't know what we can do."

There was a long pause.

"Miss Townsend?"

"I'm sorry . . ."

"Are you all right?"

Katherine sighed, tried to reconnect. "Is there any chance he's at a friend's nearby?"

"Mr. Collins says no. The whole time he's here, he's either been with him or me. You think you could call the police and get them to help? Maybe they will listen to a government lady."

If you only knew how little power I have around here, Katherine thought. "I don't know," she answered. "I will definitely try. But I don't understand how this could happen. Did Mr. Collins do something to him?"

"No, nothing like that. There was a bit of a problem earlier, before dark. Mr. Collins said some mean things—that wooden soldier thing came up—but I don't think it was enough to make Patrick run away. The only thing that makes any sense to me is Patrick must have seen the telegram."

Katherine heard words in the background. "Mr. Collins is saying that's impossible. But it's the only thing that makes sense." There was a scratching sound, and then: "Listen, old man, you don't know anything. We both know you were drunk . . . I'm not blaming you, I'm just saying when I left you, you headed back to the dining room, staring at a whiskey bottle, and the telegram was on the table. How do you know Patrick didn't see it?" A pause, then: "That's right, you don't."

"Mrs. Fortini, why wouldn't Patrick call me? I gave him my card and told him all he had to do was call me and I would rush right over."

"I don't know, Miss Townsend—"

"Please call me Katherine."

"Okay, Katherine. Maybe he was afraid Mr. Collins would find out. I'm on his phone now, and it's just a few feet away from the dining room table where he was sitting when I brought Patrick home."

"Then why didn't he come to you?"

"I don't know that, either. We've never had a cross moment.

I've made it very clear to Patrick I'm totally on his side. He's come to me before when he got upset. I can't think of why he wouldn't come to me now."

Katherine was trying to sound professional, ask all the right questions, uncover the facts, but inside . . . she felt at any moment she might lose it completely. "How is Mr. Collins doing?"

"Let me move into the kitchen." Mrs. Fortini was whispering now. "He's a wreck. Keeps saying 'It's all my fault, all my fault' over and over. I've never seen him like this, not even when Ida died. And he's convinced Shawn is dead, not missing. Now he's sure Patrick is next. To tell you the truth, I can't blame him. I'm trying to keep calm, but . . . I don't know. Have you seen what it's like outside? Halfway from his house to mine, I didn't think I could take another step."

"Well, let's see what happens if I call the police myself. I wish I could think of some way to get them to care. Have you tried calling the fire department?"

"Not yet."

"Well, give me both numbers if you have them, and I'll call them right now."

"Hey . . . I just thought of something."

"What?"

"Just a minute . . . hey, Mr. Collins." Mrs. Fortini was yelling off to the side. "You've got some money around here, don't you?" Katherine waited a few moments, then heard: "I don't mean in your wallet, I'm talking about some real money, big money. Didn't you make a lot of money when you sold your business a few years ago?"

Katherine couldn't make out what Collins said but definitely heard a verbal reaction on the other end.

"Katherine, I think we might have an idea. Mr. Collins tells me he's got money enough to burn. He's up off his chair right now, said he's got money stashed all around this house. I think we might have a way to motivate these men to start looking for Patrick. We'll offer them a reward."

"You think he's got enough money to make a difference? He didn't seem like a man who had—"

"I don't know how much he has, but I know he's got more than he lets on. I've seen little hints of it over the years. Let me ask him to guess how much we're talking about. That way you could tell the police and firemen there's a cash reward for anyone who finds Patrick. This time of year, everyone needs extra money. You want me to call you back?"

"No, I'll hold."

Katherine hoped it might be at least five hundred dollars, though that seemed unlikely. She didn't know what policemen made but guessed it couldn't be much more than two or three hundred a month. A couple months free salary at Christmastime might just be enough to get a few cops willing to pull away from the fireplace.

"Katherine, you're not going to believe this. Mr. Collins says you can tell them he'll put up a five-thousand-dollar reward for Patrick's safe return!"

"Is that even possible?"

"I'm looking at . . . at least three thousand dollars cash right now sitting on the dining room table, and Ian says that's just from the first two places he's looked. He said if we need to offer more, he's got more money than he can count in the bank."

Katherine couldn't believe it. The old man was rich. "I'll call them right away and get back with you as soon as I can."

Katherine hung up the phone after talking to the fire chief in the little township where Ian Collins lived. Before that,

she'd been talking with the captain of the municipal police. Both were now very interested in looking for Patrick. First she had to convince them this was no hoax and that the five thousand dollars really did exist. She gave the men Collins's address and said they could both send someone over right away to verify the amount.

She also had to swear that she wouldn't leak a word about the reward money to the press. Both men made it clear the search parties were being assembled now and would be sent out within the hour, but only because it was the right thing to do. The money part—if it became known—would cause everyone to get the wrong idea, like they were *only* doing it for the money. Surely she could understand how that would look.

Katherine understood perfectly.

But no matter. Help was on the way, the first real hope injected into this dismal situation. The only thing she insisted was that they send someone over to pick her up and drive her to Collins's home. She'd go insane just sitting there doing nothing with Patrick out lost in the cold.

Thirty

Rummaging through the trash for food. His humiliation was now complete.

Two days out from Christmas and now he'd been laid off his job, for no good reason. 'Cept his rich white boss said he don't need no driver no more. What, he going to drive his big Caddy around by himself? Ezra Jeffries wasn't no fool. He heard what the folks 'round the house'd been whispering, the other hired help working for the Radcliffes. They all say Mr. Radcliffe gonna fire your butt before Christmas day, and they right. They say Mr. Radcliffe gonna give his job to some old white friend's out-a-work nephew, or some other thing.

Things no better here for the black man than they'd been in the Carolinas. He only been up here four months, got the tip on this job from his cousin Alvin, who worked next door from the Radcliffe place. Since then, Ezra never miss a day, never been late, never let a scratch get on that car. Always keep it clean, shiny as a top, say, "Yes, sir" and "No, sir," even, "As you wish, sir," something the butler said rich white folk like to hear. He gave him the paper every morning, got that door open 'fore he even had to ask. They never once complain about the way Ezra worked, not even once. Then . . . they just let him go, just like that. Two days out from Christmas.

Now, what he gonna do?

Ezra had four mouths to feed. His wife Ruby's paycheck didn't barely cover the rent, and that was due the week after Christmas. He just spent his last bit of money buying one Christmas present each for Ruby and their two kids. Now he don't even have enough cash to buy food. So here he is, out in the freezing cold and snow, maybe a mile from home, digging in trash boxes like some old tomcat.

Ruby'd been getting on him about all his complaining, said we gotta trust the Lord for the good and bad come our way, but, "Jesus," he said, looking up, "I'd sure like to see just a little more good, if you please." About the only good thing he could say going on here now was no one out walking around in weather like this, see him fumbling through the trash this way.

It was plenty dark down the alley and plenty cold. But he figured the cold and snow might just be his friend. It got all the stores to close early tonight, and the weatherman say this storm might keep 'em closed another day or two, maybe even till Christmas. He figured that might cause the grocery men to be putting food out in the trash tonight that still was fit to eat, the cold might keep it from going bad.

Judging by all these boxes piled up in the alley next to Hodgins's Grocery, Ezra had it figured just about right. He passed by this store every day on his way back to the Radcliffe estate. He might just get lucky and find something they could all eat that didn't look like it came from the trash.

He hadn't told Ruby about losing his job yet, couldn't see worrying her so close to Christmas. She worked so hard every day, first cleaning her white folks' place, then coming home to clean theirs. And he knew she'd make him take back the

Christmas present he'd bought her and buy food. But no way Ezra would. He couldn't get a present for her last year and still hated the feeling he got every time he thought on it.

As he opened the lid to the first box he came to, he noticed the snow was up past his ankles now, coming down real hard. He maybe only had one or two hours at most to do what he came here to do and get back home, 'fore he got himself stuck out here in the snow.

The first box was just full of smaller boxes and old newspapers. He set it aside and went after the bigger box underneath. Now this looked promising. It had several loaves of bread and two bags of odd-sized rolls. He had to take his gloves off to check, but two of the loaves hadn't hardened up yet. He emptied out the first box and put them inside. "Give us this day our daily bread," he mumbled.

Moving on to the box underneath, he almost gagged as he opened the lid. It looked full of newspapers, but it stank like rotting fish. He closed the lid quickly and set it aside.

Just then, he heard a strange noise.

He stopped and looked about. Couldn't see no one. But it sounded like somebody moaning. Maybe just the wind, he thought. He walked out to the edge of the alley and looked down the street.

Instantly, the snow and wind slapped him in the face, and he pulled back. But he didn't see a soul. He rushed back to the pile of boxes, moved the first row aside, and got to work on the next. The first box in the second row brought a big smile to his face. It was full of cans. All dented and mangled but none of them open.

He held each one up to a dim light by the side door. Some labels were too ripped to read, but he found two decent cans of green beans, a big can of corn, and three cans of chicken soup. Now this was somethin'. If he stopped now, they'd have at least one good dinner and a passable lunch. After putting them in the box with the bread, he decided to keep going. No telling if this storm would let him out of the house again once he quit.

There was that noise again.

He could tell it was coming from farther down the alley, not the street. It wasn't a cat or a dog; it was something bigger. "Who's there?" he yelled. "Who's back there?"

No one answered.

He looked around and saw an old wooden pallet. He broke a board off, held it up like a bat. "You better answer me," he yelled, walking slowly in that general direction. "I don't want to hurt you, but I will if I have to."

Still no answer. He stood there a few moments but heard only the wind. He turned back toward the boxes, took one step and, there, there it was again. He spun around. "All right, now, I know somebody's back here." He swung the board back and forth.

He heard the moaning sound once more, but this close he could tell it was low, down by the pavement. And it sounded more like a child, like one of his kids with a sour stomach. He squatted down and talked a little softer. "Are you hurt? Somebody hurt you? 'Cause I ain't here to hurt you." He waited a few moments. "Where are you?"

Still no answer. He put the board down now and moved slowly toward the sound. The back of the alley was darker, but his eyes were starting to adjust. He could just make out a few large boxes leaning up against a fence. He thought he saw something moving in the corner by the biggest one. He reached out his hand, praying it wasn't a bad dog or some old crazy man gonna jump out and attack him.

"I ain't gonna hurt you none," he said. "You okay?"

There was no reply, but his hand felt the arm of an overcoat. He gently squeezed and could tell it was the arm of a child. "Hey," he said softly. "Are you okay? What you doing out here all alone?"

The child did not answer. He felt his way toward its head. It was wearing a hat and scarf, but it was trembling all over. Just then, it moaned again.

"Good Lord," he said. "What a child doing out here at a time like this?"

✑

About ten minutes later, Ezra had the situation sized up. But it didn't look good.

Bad enough he was out here in the snow snooping for food in the trash, but now he got this little frozen white boy to worry about. He couldn't get the boy to wake up, his little mouth be chattering something fierce. He held him tight, trying to get him warm, but it was no good. His whole body was still trembling. He had to get him out of this place but quick. He tucked him back against the big box and walked out to the edge of the alley. Still not a soul in sight.

He went back and picked up the boy, tucked him in his right arm, and carried him to the box of food he'd been working on. He tried picking it up with his free hand, see if he could carry them both, but it was just no use. Ezra was strong, but with this storm, he knew he'd drop one or the other before he made it two blocks down the road.

Of all the crazy fool things . . . How was he gonna explain this to Ruby? What if anybody saw him carrying some white boy around out here in this storm? How he gonna explain that, and who was gonna believe what he said?

He set the boy down again and started shoving cans in his coat pockets, any opening he could find. He tucked the boy tightly against his flannel shirt, then wrapped his coat around him and buttoned him inside. Look as big as Alvin now, he thought. He wondered how he gonna carry all this weight back to their apartment. In the middle of a storm, no less.

But if he left the boy to get help, he'd surely be dead before he get back. He got to the edge of the alley, took one look back—maybe saying good-bye to all that food—then stepped into the icy wind.

It was way worse than he figured. Even with the streetlights on, he couldn't see fifty feet in front of him. The snow on the sidewalk was up past his shins in spots, past his knees in others. He pulled his scarf up to cover his face, leaned forward, and started walking.

"One foot in front of the other," he said. "That's how we gonna do this."

Thirty-One

As Katherine pulled up to Collins's home, she noticed another squad car parked outside, and then another car she later learned belonged to a lieutenant with the fire department. Once inside, there were four men gathered around the dining room table, going over a map of the area. Probably planning their strategy, she thought.

Mrs. Fortini and Mr. Collins were both sitting in the living room. Collins looked straight ahead, staring at the wall. Mrs. Fortini instantly rose to greet her, gave her a big hug. "Miss Townsend, I'm so glad you're here."

"Katherine, remember?" she said, still in the grip of the hug.

"Katherine, yes. Come in, let me get your coat. You want some coffee, hot chocolate? I made both."

"Some coffee would be great. Any word on Patrick? Anything at all?"

"No, but there were at least ten men here just a few minutes before you arrived. They're out now looking in different sections of the neighborhood. And these other men at the table are about to join them, searching around the business district. There's another man in the kitchen on the phone, talking with the Transit Authority. He's seeing if there's any chance Patrick may have taken a bus."

"A bus? By himself?"

"I know," said Mrs. Fortini. "Doesn't seem likely a bus driver would let a boy that small get on without an adult. I didn't argue. I'm just glad they're finally doing something."

"Do they know about the apartment on Clark Street?" Katherine asked. "Think there's any chance Patrick would have tried to go back home?"

"Mr. Collins told the man on the phone about it. He said they'd send a car there just in case."

Then Katherine remembered the first night she brought Patrick here and told him he could call her anytime, day or night, that he didn't even need his grandfather's permission. What if Patrick was out in the snow trying to find her? What if he left the house to find a telephone, someplace he could call her without Collins finding out? But there was no one at the office now, and she wasn't at home.

The front door opened, letting in a surge of cold air. Everyone instantly looked up. Just another policeman, his hat and shoulders covered in snow. He looked past them to the officers in the dining room. "No sign of him yet. It's slow going, but we've already scoured three blocks in every direction."

"Tell 'em to keep at it," one of the officers said. "He couldn't have gone far."

Another officer came out of the kitchen and added, "No sign of him on Clark Street, sir. Harrison said he knocked on all the neighbor apartments; no one has seen a little boy out and about since the storm began. And the Transit people heard back from those two bus drivers, the ones made their last runs within a few blocks of here. Neither one reported seeing a little boy get on. Dead ends all around, I'm afraid."

The man she guessed was the captain made a face at the

officer, pointing with his head in the direction of the living room. The officer seemed to get the message. "But I'm sure he'll turn up soon, it's just a matter of time."

Katherine looked at Mrs. Fortini, then at Collins. They all got the first message. This wasn't looking good.

༚

Collins decided he just couldn't sit there anymore. He needed an occupation, something, anything to get his mind off the growing dread inside. Every single one of the men involved in the search, at one time or another as they walked by, shot him a look that said: "So, you're the one drove this little boy out into the cold." The angry comebacks, so easy to dish out on any other day, just weren't there. Because it was true. He *was* the reason Patrick was missing, the only reason. He couldn't sit there anymore and absorb the stares, didn't have the energy to resist the thoughts behind them.

Mrs. Fortini hadn't said a cross word to him, though she had every right. Even the Townsend woman seemed to look at him with more sympathy than disgust. But he felt enough disgust inside to make up for them both. He stood up, almost startling the women.

"Where you going, Ian?" Mrs. Fortini asked.

"I don't know, maybe I'm just stretching."

"You want any coffee?"

"No thanks."

What he wanted to do was just put on his coat and boots and head outside to help. But the police captain had forbidden it. "Besides," he'd said, "you need to be here to greet Patrick when we bring him home."

But Collins knew . . . his face was the last face Patrick would want to see if—*when*—he walked through that door.

Then it came to him. He suddenly knew exactly what face Patrick *would* want to see.

The wooden soldier.

He would go up right now and get it down from the attic. No . . . better yet, he would stay up in the attic and finish carving the soldier, even paint it.

"Where you going?" Mrs. Fortini asked.

"Something I've gotta do," he replied. "May be upstairs awhile. You keep things running down here for me? Get the men whatever they need?"

"You mean like I've been doing since I got here?"

Collins smiled.

So that was the plan. He would finish the wooden soldier in Shawn's honor and have it done before Patrick came home. And he would give it to Patrick as his Christmas present.

He may not have a way with words, but he knew how to carve right well.

Thirty-Two

Ezra moved more by instinct now than sense. He couldn't feel his fingers or toes, but he could still feel the boy under his coat, and his legs were still pushing through the snow. The streetlights were out on his block, but he found his way by the odd light shining here and there through the tenement windows.

He looked up through the wind and snow and could just see on the left the turnoff to his apartment, an alley much like the one back at Hodgins's Grocery. 'Cept his alley led up a rickety flight of wooden steps to three rooms and a bathroom they shared with a couple next door.

Ruby would be worried something fierce 'bout now, he figured. Get to that place where he better be dead or she'd kill him for making her fret so. But he reckoned she'd stop being sore soon as she laid eyes on the boy. She might be right proud of him for saving his sorry life.

Man, but he was cold. Every muscle in his legs and arms felt like they might just pop loose any minute. At least the boy wasn't shaking as bad as when they first started out. *Hope he ain't dead*, Ezra thought. He stayed as close to the walls as he could, cut down on the wind. Just a little ways to go now. He sure hoped Ruby got that heat going. That radiator upstairs mooed like a small cow, but it would be music to his ears at this point.

As he rounded the corner into their alley, he looked up at the window overlooking the stairs. There she was, his Ruby staring down at him. Her brown shawl wrapped around her shoulders, arms crossed. Didn't look like she'd seen him, but she was looking.

The snow was up past the second step. He steadied himself on the rail, trying to clear it with his foot, but his foot felt like a wooden club about now. He stomped down a few times, trying to get some feeling back. Ruby must have heard him. She flung that front door open quick as you please. The wind caught it, and it slammed against the back wall.

"Ezra, that you? Please be you," she cried.

"It's me, darlin', I'm all right. Colder than I ever been in my life, but I'm all right." She started climbing down to meet him. "Now you get back in the living room, darlin'. You ain't dressed for this. I'll be up directly." She obeyed, and he could hear her crying over the sound of the wind.

"Your daddy's home, boys. God brung him back just like we prayed."

Ezra made it to the last step. *Just one more deep breath*, he told himself, *just one more will do it*. The next thing he knew he was safe inside. He dropped to his knees and feared he might drop right over, crushing the little boy under his weight. Ruby closed the door. "Open my coat, Ruby, would you please? I can't even move my arms."

She was on him in a flash, hugging and holding him tight. So were his two boys, all wrapped around him like a rope. "Daddy, you're so big," his youngest, Joseph, said. "You got presents in there for us?" Joseph pointed to his coat. "Christmas presents?"

Ruby started unbuttoning his jacket. "Afraid not," he said. "But wait till you see——" Before he finished, the little boy plopped out of his coat and fell to the floor.

"Good gracious, Ezra."

"We gotta get him warmed up right quick," Ezra said. "Is he breathin'? Check and see if he's breathin'.'"

"Where'd you get him?" she asked as she cradled him in her arms. She put her hand over his chest. "Heart beatin' all right, nice and strong. What happened? Where'd he come from?"

Ezra's two boys backed away toward the edge of the room, eyes fixed hard on this little stranger come into their home. "Long story, Ruby. I'll tell you the whole thing you get me something hot to drink. I need to get him and me over by that radiator." It wasn't putting out strong heat, but it felt good as a fireplace right now. He smiled as he heard it moan and hiss.

"Boys, go get the blankets off the bed, put them on your daddy and this little boy." Ruby walked toward the kitchen. "I already got hot water on the stove, have you some nice hot tea in just a minute. I'm so glad you're home."

Ezra leaned his back against the radiator and pulled the boy up on his lap. As soon as his boys returned, he wrapped the boy in the first blanket, then himself. "You boys yank these boots off your daddy? The little boy's too."

"Yessir," they both said, and took to it like a wartime mission.

Ruby came in from the kitchen a few minutes later, carrying a hot cup of tea. "Okay, Ezra. Now you tell me what's going on here, and how you come to have this boy."

He looked to his boys stacking the wet boots by the front door. "I will, Ruby. Just give me a few seconds here to catch my breath. You boys . . . I'm gonna need a few minutes with your mama. You head off to your bedroom, now."

"We gotta get to bed?" said Willy, the oldest. "Can't we hear the story?"

"It's way past your bedtime already," Ruby said. "I only let you stay up to wait on your daddy. Well, he's home now, so you go on. I'll be there in a few minutes to say your prayers." And off they went.

She picked the two overcoats off the floor. "Now what we got here," she said, holding his up. "What you got in here?" She started pulling the food out of his pockets. "What in the—"

"I'll explain, Ruby. Come over here and sit by me. I don't want the boys hearing what I gotta say."

She reached down and put her hand across the white boy's forehead. "Don't feel no fever. What's his name?"

"I don't know. He hasn't opened his eyes or said a word since I found him."

"He unconscious?"

"I think he's just sleeping. I think he'll be okay come morning."

Ruby sat on the chair closest to the radiator, looked back at the collection of food he brought home on the table, then down at the boy again. "Okay, Ezra. Start talking."

Ezra knew he'd have to tell her everything. She'd like the hero part, about him finding and saving this here boy. But then he'd have to tell her where he found the boy and where this food came from. Dread filled his heart as he thought about the hardest part of the tale, the part where he lost his job. What an awful night this was for his poor Ruby. She'd gone from fretting something awful to joy at his return. And now he was about to plunge her right back into fretting once again.

And that only two days out from Christmas.

Thirty-Three

Collins awoke disoriented. He was in his bed, had a terrific headache, and was still in his clothes. He was lying on top of the bedspread, not under it. And he was cold, so cold. The amount of light coming in the window suggested midmorning, at least. What was going on? He sat up slowly as the events of the night before began to come together in his mind.

Patrick, where was Patrick?

Then he remembered. He was gone.

He remembered working in the attic until 1:00 a.m. carving the wooden soldier, when the police captain called up to him from the second floor. The captain said they were calling off the search until daylight. His men had covered ten square blocks around the house, but no sign of Patrick. The only thing that made any sense is that someone took Patrick in for the night. Come morning, he'd have the men start going house to house. They were sure he'd turn up. Collins wanted to believe him, but he didn't sound very convincing.

The captain also informed him two officers had escorted Mrs. Fortini and Miss Townsend next door for the night, and that he'd leave an officer downstairs, in case something unexpected turned up.

After the captain left, Collins had gone back upstairs to finish the wooden soldier. He didn't know how long he'd been at it, but he worked until it was done. Then he came down and collapsed on his bed.

All he needed now was to go back up and paint it. If they did find Patrick today, Collins wanted the soldier completely finished and waiting by the front door. He put on a fresh shirt and noticed out the window that the storm had stopped. The trees were still, the winds had ceased. The snow had blanketed his entire street, smoothing away all the hard edges.

Directly below he saw deep footprints leading away from the house, but he didn't see any officers standing or moving around outside. He looked up and down the street; not a soul was in sight. *Where the heck are they?* he thought. *Should be guys all up and down the street, knocking on doors and searching backyards.*

As he buttoned his shirt, he made his way downstairs. Someone had better explain why no one was out looking for his grandson.

∽

Katherine Townsend had slept but not well. She never slept well when not in her own bed, but all the more with so much on her mind. Last night, Mrs. Fortini had made her something she called a "hot toddy" to help quiet her nerves. It didn't work. She saw her make it with brandy and lemon, and wanted to tell her to just give her the brandy, keep the lemon.

She got up from the bed and began changing from a borrowed nightgown to the clothes she'd worn yesterday. A look out the window revealed the storm had ended, but she was shocked at the amount of snow on the ground. It was halfway up her car door. The next shock was that her car was the only car out front, at either house.

Where were the policemen and firemen from last night? The officer who'd helped them over to Mrs. Fortini's said they'd all be back at first light. She looked at a clock on the nightstand. It was 9:30 already.

All right, don't get mad, she told herself. Maybe they had already come and were out searching on a different block. But then she looked again. The snow in front of the house and out by the street was undisturbed.

Now she was getting mad.

She took a quick look in the dresser mirror, brushed her hair a few strokes, then heard someone humming softly in the kitchen. "Mrs. Fortini?"

"Oh, there you are, Katherine. Care for some coffee?"

"Huh? Yes, that would be nice. Do you know what's going on? It's after 9:30, and I don't see anything going on out front."

"Now, you just sit down over there, and I'll make you a couple of eggs and toast."

"I'm sorry, I don't think I can eat. I don't understand why isn't anyone out looking for Patrick."

"In a way, they are," she said, almost smiling. "I've already talked with the police captain almost two hours ago. I decided not to wake you. There really isn't anything more either of us can do."

"I don't understand."

"The captain explained a plan they came up with for this morning, and I had to admit, it sounded like a good plan to me." She set the cup of coffee down in front of her.

"Okay, I'm listening."

"He said the storm brought way more snow than anyone predicted, and it would take his men the better part of a day just to see the houses within a few blocks of here. The cars are all snowed in. You like your eggs fried or scrambled?"

"What?"

"Fried or scrambled?"

"Scrambled is fine."

"Anyway, someone had the idea to call everyone. Almost all the homes around here have telephones now. The phone company gave them the numbers of each house, street by street. So he's put his men on phone duty. The same men who were out searching last night are now calling each house in the neighborhood to see if anyone took Patrick in."

Katherine smiled. It actually was a good idea. "Did he say how long it would take?"

"He didn't know; they've never done anything like this before. But he sounded very optimistic."

"Maybe I could help. I'm good on the phone."

"Katherine, have you looked outside? We're snowed in. Your car is almost buried, and the streets are completely covered."

Katherine sighed. "It's just so hard to sit here doing nothing."

"We're not doing nothing. We're having a nice breakfast together."

"You seem so . . ." She didn't want to accuse her of not caring. "Relaxed."

"In a way, I guess I am. I don't know what you think about these things, but when I woke up this morning and said my prayers, I got a very strong feeling that everything was going to be okay. I don't think God is going to take Patrick away from us. He knows how much we can handle, and none of us could handle losing him right now. Least of all Mr. Collins next door."

Katherine had a hard time imagining God would do anything out of the ordinary to help that old man. "I wish I felt as secure about this as you."

Mrs. Fortini just smiled. "Here you go."

She set a nice plate of scrambled eggs and toast in front of her. That and the coffee did seem to quiet her nerves. "Maybe I better call the office, let them know what's happened."

"You could," said Mrs. Fortini, "but the radio said the whole town is pretty much shut down from the storm. Tell you what you could do, if you have the energy, that is."

"Anything."

"I've got a snow shovel in the basement. Maybe after you eat, could you make a small path between here and next door? Just wide enough for our feet. I'd like to check in on Mr. Collins if we could."

What a sweet woman, Katherine thought. When she thought of Collins, the best she could manage was a momentary suppression of rage. "I'd be happy to do that, Mrs. Fortini. The eggs are wonderful, by the way."

"Glad you like them."

"I hope we hear something soon. I don't know if I can make it through a whole day without knowing where Patrick is, if he's doing all right."

"Well, let me turn on the radio and see if that helps. They're supposed to be playing Christmas music all day. Tomorrow is Christmas Eve, you know."

Thirty-Four

"I think he's waking up."

"Is he?"

"I think so. Hey, little boy, you okay?"

Patrick felt very strange. He heard a pleasant woman's voice but didn't recognize it. He tried to focus, but nothing looked familiar. "Where am I?"

"You're at our place," the woman said. "You had a terrible time last night. You remember anything?"

Patrick looked up into the smiling face of a colored woman. Beside her was a big colored man, smiling just as much. Then he heard some giggles.

"You boys stay back," the man said. "Give him some space, now."

Patrick looked to the left of the woman and saw two little colored boys, one about his age, the other a little older. "What's your name?" the older boy asked.

"Patrick. Patrick Collins."

"I told you he looked Irish," the man said.

"Oh, Ezra. Like you so smart," the woman said. "Over half the folks where you found him be Irish. You hungry,

Patrick? We let you sleep till you get up on your own. It's past lunchtime, but we saved you some food."

Patrick looked around. It looked like the living room of his apartment on Clark Street, only smaller. And there were no rugs on the floor, and the furniture looked much older and worn. "I guess so," he answered. But he wasn't sure what colored folks ate. He had never met any before. His mom had told him about them, how some people treated them badly because they were different. But she said they were just people like us, and God loves everyone the same.

"You want to go outside and play?" the boy his age asked. "Snowed all last night. We could make a snowman."

Patrick loved making snowmen. "I guess so."

"Now, you wait a little while," the woman said to the boy. "Let's let Patrick have a few minutes to eat and get situated."

"But it'll get dark in just a few hours," the boy said.

"Mind your mama," said the man. "Say, Patrick, how you come to be in that alley last night, by Hodgins's Grocery? Don't you got any kin?"

"They must be worried something awful," the woman said.

Patrick didn't want to talk about it. He looked up at the woman. "What's your name?"

"Me? I'm Ruby, and this here is Ezra, my husband. Over there is Joseph, and Willy, our oldest."

"Do you have a last name?"

She laughed. "It's Jeffries."

"How did I get here, Mrs. Jeffries?"

"I brung you here last night," Ezra said. "Found you in that alley. Look like you were half dead. You remember how you got there?"

"I was waiting for a bus, but it never came. Then it got so cold. All the stores were closed. The alley was the only place I could go."

"You don't have a home?" Mrs. Jeffries asked.

Patrick hesitated, trying to think of what to say. "I guess I was running away."

"Why?" Mr. Jeffries asked. "And on a night like that, of all nights."

"I don't know."

"Well, whatever the problem is, I'm sure your mama must be worried sick about now. She won't know if you dead or alive, I expect."

Patrick started to cry, he couldn't help it. "My mom is already dead," he said. "In a car wreck, a week ago."

"Oh my Lord."

"What about your daddy?" asked Mr. Jeffries.

"He's away at the war; people are trying to find him." Then Patrick remembered the telegram and started crying even harder. "But he's missing. They don't even know where he is," he said through his tears.

"My, my," Mrs. Jeffries said. She wrapped her arms around his head and drew him near. "You go ahead and cry if you need to, Patrick. I expect I'd be crying myself if I were you. Have half a mind to join you."

"But where you staying?" asked Mr. Jeffries. "Somebody must have been lookin' after you."

Patrick heard him but didn't want to answer. He'd rather stay here with the Jeffries than go back to his grandfather's. Then he remembered the card Miss Townsend had given him. "I don't want to go back to where I was staying. But there's a nice government lady we could call. She was the one I was trying to see last night. Could we call her now? Her name's Miss Townsend."

Both of them made a sad face. "I wish we could," said Mrs. Jeffries, "but we don't have a telephone."

"We're gettin' one soon," Mr. Jeffries said, "but we just moved up a few months ago from the Carolinas."

Mrs. Jeffries gave him a funny look. "Maybe we could call down at the store on the corner, though. Do you know her number?"

"It's on a card in my coat pocket."

"I don't know, Ruby. All that snow, I'm thinking no stores be open today. Maybe for a few days."

"I know someone's got a phone," said Willy. "A boy I was playing with on the next block. His folks got one."

"How you know that?"

"He asked if we had one, said he wanted to call me after the storm, see if we could come out and play."

"You know where he lives?" asked Mr. Jeffries.

"Yep. Right where. Just the next block over."

Mr. Jeffries looked at Mrs. Jeffries. "We could do that then, Ruby. Me and Willy can go right now, while the boy eats and gets situated."

"Can't I go too?" Patrick asked.

"I think you better stay here," said Mrs. Jeffries. "You had quite a time last night. I don't want you catching a cold."

"Besides," said Mr. Jeffries, "she ain't gonna be able to come get you, anyway. The streets all snowed in, and the plows don't come here till they go everywhere else. I just want to let this lady know where you are and that you're all right."

"I sure wish I could talk to her," said Patrick.

"You will, probably tomorrow," said Mrs. Jeffries. "Get you warmed up and well fed today, and they can bring you back to that telephone tomorrow, let you call her yourself."

"That would be great."

"Does that mean he can go outside and play with me?" asked Joseph. "Since Willy's going with Pa?"

"We'll see about that," said Mrs. Jeffries. "Let's let Patrick eat, and see how things go after that."

Patrick didn't know what to make of all this. All he knew was that he already felt much better here than he had the whole time at his grandfather's. And Miss Townsend would know where he was in a little while, and maybe tomorrow he would see her. He knew once she heard all that happened, she would take him away from his grandfather for good.

Maybe he could even live with her.

Thirty-Five

Ezra hated coming back home to Ruby with more bad news. Willy didn't mind it a bit. Kids always have it easy like that. Their minds just skip to the next thing, so easy to see the bright side.

Took almost forty minutes to get to Willy's friend's place, the snow being so high. He told them this little white boy's sad story, and they were happy to let him use their phone. He called this Miss Townsend from that card, and let it ring till the operator said he gotta hang up. Nobody answered, either at the office number or the number she wrote on back. He waited a whole hour, called four different times, just so Ruby and Patrick would know he did his best. But nobody ever answered.

He had to get back now, before it get completely dark.

Now it was even colder than before. About the only consolation was he and Willy could walk through the same path in the snow they'd made getting here. But now, he just gonna walk forty more minutes in the cold, just to say it was all a waste of time.

"Say, Pa. You know what day tomorrow is, right?"

"Yes, I do, Willy."

"It's Christmas Eve, Pa. Means just one more day, then Christmas."

"I know, son. Let's keep moving. We ain't got time for you to be stoppin' and lookin' in all these store windows."

And Ezra didn't need reminding of all the other things he couldn't afford for his family.

"Okay, Pa."

❦

Sadness had descended with the setting sun on the Collins's home this night.

Katherine had just gotten off the phone with the police captain and had to inform Mr. Collins and Mrs. Fortini that all the homes within the search area with telephones had been contacted, and no one had taken in a little boy.

It was as if Patrick had simply vanished.

The only sliver of hope that remained was that Patrick might have been taken in by the forty or so homes in the neighborhood that didn't have telephones. The captain said his men had the lists made up and planned to go knocking on all these doors first thing tomorrow morning, even though it was Christmas Eve. He still spoke with confidence about finding Patrick.

But where could he have gone?

She looked away from the window at the wooden soldier centered on the coffee table. Katherine had to admit, the elder Collins was a gifted artist. The level of detail in both the wood carving and paint was astonishing. This soldier was worthy of a shelf in any museum or gallery she had ever seen. When he had come down from the attic an hour ago and set it down on the table, he just said, "This should do it."

It really did seem like something had changed inside him. Comparing how harsh he'd been since the night she first met him, then seeing the look on his face after learning Patrick had disappeared . . . She couldn't hate him anymore. He was clearly as upset, if not more, than she was.

He had now resumed a slouched position in his chair, staring blankly at the wall like yesterday. Mrs. Fortini was busying herself in the kitchen, making them all some dinner. Katherine could tell she was bothered by the lack of news, but not shaken. Katherine thought it must be nice to have a place like that to go to in your mind, to have faith. She, however, was a realist. She'd found it better, especially since taking this job, to keep her expectations low, since life consistently met them, and rarely exceeded them. But with Patrick, she couldn't let her heart give up hope. They had to find him. He had to be all right.

"Who's ready for dinner?" Mrs. Fortini called from the dining room. "I made you spaghetti and my world-famous meatballs. I think we need spaghetti on a night like this." She walked back into the kitchen.

"I'd love some spaghetti," Katherine replied, not sure if she could even eat anything right now. "Mr. Collins . . . ready for dinner?" He didn't move. She tapped him on the shoulder. "Want some spaghetti?"

"Huh . . . spaghetti?"

He looked up, but it was as if his eyes looked past her. She saw such despair in those eyes, such deep sadness. "Maybe some good cooking will cheer us up."

He sat up. "I guess so." He glanced over at the wooden soldier on the table, then at the front door. He buried his face in his hands, but just for a moment, then stood up. "I'll be right there."

Katherine obliged and walked toward the dining room without him but looked back at him over her shoulder. He walked over to the wooden soldier and picked it up. He held it about chest high, turning it once on its side as if to catch its profile, then set it back on the table facing the front door. He walked to the front window and parted the curtains slightly. She sat down at the table as Mrs. Fortini came out with some rolls.

"What's he doing?" she whispered.

"I don't know," said Katherine.

"Poor man."

Collins turned around, and they both quickly looked at each other.

"Okay, let's eat," he said as he walked into the dining room.

"Anything I can help you with, Mrs. Fortini?" Katherine asked.

"Maybe just pour us each a nice glass of Chianti. Is that okay, Ian? I brought a bottle with me when we came over this afternoon."

"I like a good Chianti with spaghetti," he said as he sat down.

Once the food and bread were dished out and the wine glasses filled, Collins said, "Okay if I say grace tonight?"

It surprised Katherine but clearly shocked Mrs. Fortini. "Fine, Ian. That would be just fine."

∽

After Collins prayed, he took a large helping of spaghetti and meatballs from Mrs. Fortini. He was glad he remembered the right words to pray; it had been awhile. He didn't fully understand what had come over him, but he definitely felt something shifting inside. It actually seemed to happen as he held the wooden soldier in his hands.

He'd been so busy working on it the last twenty-four hours, and prior to that could only connect it to a myriad of conflicting emotions. He'd never allowed himself to see the wooden soldier for what it was, or what it represented. Here was a man taking charge of a situation in the midst of great peril, giving no thought to his own life or safety. A man doing his duty. A Collins always does his duty. Somehow getting clear on this got through to him just now. He couldn't just sit there anymore wallowing in doubt and this paralyzing fear. He had a job to do. His job was to keep focused and prepared for Patrick's return. It was pointless to let his mind dwell on the hopeless scenario that Patrick was lost to him for good.

So they didn't find him today. They would keep looking tomorrow. And if not tomorrow, then the day after that, and the day after that. But it was his duty to make sure they did find Patrick and that he was ready to care for Patrick properly when he did return.

"Another roll, Mrs. Fortini, if you please."

Thirty-Six

It was Christmas Eve morning.

Ezra Jeffries's two boys had come running in to wake him early, just to make sure he knew. He was sitting down now at their little wooden table in the kitchen, drinking a cup of coffee with Ruby, still in her robe, watching his boys and Patrick play marbles on the living room floor.

Last night when Ezra got home, Patrick took the news pretty good about him not getting through to the government lady. He let Ruby do the telling, and by the time she through explaining things to Patrick, he not only didn't cry, he was smilin' like it wasn't bad news at all.

Now Ezra was thinking other thoughts about the plan they came up with, sitting here with his coffee, watching the boys play, hoping by the end of the day he wasn't gonna get beat up or, worse, thrown in jail. He didn't tell Ruby about what he feared, but he knew a little bit more about how white folks could get when they saw a black man doing something they didn't understand. Like walking around with a white boy in a white neighborhood, a boy who been lost out in the snow a couple of days.

But the plan called for Ezra bringing Patrick back home

himself, since there didn't seem to be any other way to connect with this government lady named Townsend. Ruby had to promise Patrick they wouldn't bring him back to the grandpa but to some nice lady who lived next door.

"Say, Patrick," said Ezra, "I think it be time to start getting ready for our walk."

"Can't we finish our game, Pa?" said Willy. "Just a few more minutes?"

"Afraid not, son. We got a long walk to get him back, and the snow still blockin' the whole way. And I want to get back home myself before dark. We got our own things to do tonight, remember? What night is it?"

"Christmas Eve!" both boys shouted.

"That's right. So you turn him loose and let him get ready."

After Patrick got dressed and bundled up, Ezra hugged his boys and gave Ruby a kiss, hoping badly he would be back in her arms by the end of this day. His boys and Patrick hugged each other like they already best friends. *Kids got it so easy that way*, he thought. "Okay, Patrick, let's be goin', now."

As they made their way out to the street, Patrick immediately took hold of Ezra's hand. There weren't too many people out walking around, but they were all colored folk, and he wasn't too worried about the stares he'd be getting in this neighborhood. It was plenty cold, but the wind was mild. The snow hadn't melted none, but the folks already out and about had created a narrow path for them to walk in most places.

"Say, Patrick, I need to tell you something before we get to Clifton Avenue, the road where Hodgins's Grocery is. You say you know how to get home from there, right?"

"I'm pretty sure. It's only a block or so from there. I don't know the road names, but I think I can find the way."

Ezra wished he could narrow things down. Didn't want to

be asking white folk for directions once he got near Hodgins's. "Anything more you remember about the street your grandpa lives on?"

"You said we weren't going there."

"I know. But that Italian lady's on the same street, right?"

"Yes."

"You remember anything more about it, the street? Any little stores on the corner, or fire stations nearby?"

Patrick thought a moment, then said, "There's a big cemetery nearby, with a big stone wall. Mrs. Fortini took me there and lifted me up to see the graves."

"Well, that might help." But Ezra knew Allingdale had four big cemeteries nearby, going in different directions once he got to Hodgins's. That could make for an awful lot of extra walkin' till they found the right one. "Anything you remember about this cemetery? See a name at the place you go in?"

"We didn't actually go inside. But I remember one thing."

"What?"

"The graves didn't have any crosses."

"No crosses?"

"They had stars."

"Stars?"

"I didn't know what they were, but Mrs. Fortini told me. She said they were stars of David. For Jewish people."

"Ah," said Ezra. Now this made sense. "That have to be Mount Lebanon, then. I know right where that is."

"You do?"

"Yes, I do. You think you know the way if I get you to that stone wall?"

"Sure I do. Mrs. Fortini's house is right around the corner from there."

At the rate they were going, Ezra thought they might get

there in just over an hour. "Well, here's the part I got to tell you about." He stopped and bent down to talk to Patrick face-to-face. "Once we get to Clifton Avenue, the street with Hodgins's Grocery, I'm gonna have to hide you in my coat and carry you the rest of the way."

"You are? I can walk. Am I going too slow?"

"You doin' just fine. It's just . . . how can I explain this. You see, some people won't like seeing me walking with you in that neighborhood, might think . . . well, they might think I was doing something wrong."

"Why?"

How could he explain this? "See, Patrick, some white folks get nervous they see a black man walking with a white boy that don't belong to him. And I'm figurin' a lot of folks might be out looking for you, since you been gone here now two days. I wanna get you all the way to your Italian lady friend's place with no trouble. You understand what I'm saying?"

"I think so. My mom told me a little bit about this."

"That's a good boy. I'll just put you in my coat and button you up, just like the other night I brung you home. And I'll get you to that stone wall by the cemetery and you can pop your head up and we'll be right close to where you belong. That okay?"

"Sure. I don't mind."

They started walking again. Ezra felt a whole lot better now about Ruby's plan.

∽

It was just after lunchtime at the Collins house.

Although there wasn't any positive news yet about Patrick, Katherine was relieved the search teams did arrive after daybreak as promised. The men had been out looking ever since, contacting all the homes without telephones in the search area. By now, they were several blocks from Collins's home. Only two officers were left outside, stationed at the edge of the driveway.

The police captain told them this morning that the men had decided to split the five-thousand-dollar reward evenly between everyone involved in the search. Each man would still receive several hundred dollars' cash.

At the moment, she was so bored she was actually looking at pictures in one of Collins's fishing magazines. A few minutes ago, she'd called her office again. No one had answered, so at least she wasn't in trouble with Bernie Krebb.

Christmas music was playing on the radio, which helped to ease her nerves. Mrs. Fortini had suggested they turn it on a few hours ago, and Collins didn't protest. He'd gone back up into the attic about ten minutes ago. She wasn't sure why; the wooden soldier was all finished, sitting on the coffee table facing the front door.

The quiet was broken by someone coming down both sets of stairs. She looked up in time to see Collins carrying a large box. "Okay, ladies, I've got a job for you."

Mrs. Fortini came in from the kitchen as he walked into the dining room and set the box on the table. "What is this?" she asked. "Why, Ian . . ."

Katherine walked in behind him as he opened the flaps. It was filled with Christmas decorations and ornaments.

"It's Christmas Eve," he said. "It's time we set these out. You ladies mind?"

"Mind?" said Mrs. Fortini. "Ian, I don't know what to say. Ida would be so happy to see this. What's gotten into you?"

Katherine saw a tear well up in his left eye. He blinked it away, then simply said, "This is long overdue."

"I'll help," Katherine said, "but you better take the lead, Mrs. Fortini. I don't have much decorating experience."

"What do you want us to do with the tree decorations?" Mrs. Fortini asked.

"Just set them out for now. Need to get a tree first."

"Where are you going to get a tree now in all this snow?"

"I've learned something over the last few days," he said. "Money talks." He walked into the kitchen, picked up the telephone, and dialed the number the police captain had left on a notepad.

"Captain, this is Ian Collins. I know there isn't any more news. I'm calling to ask a special favor. Could you ask one of your men if they'd stop by somewhere and pick up a Christmas tree for me, bring it over this afternoon? I'm not picky. There's an extra twenty dollars in it for whoever comes. You will? Thank you. I'll be looking for him then. Good-bye."

Katherine couldn't believe what she was hearing or seeing. Christmas music, Christmas decorations, and now a Christmas tree? And instead of an angry, irritating old man, Collins was almost . . . pleasant. Whatever was happening to him, she was glad. Although, she realized it might make it difficult to follow through with her plans once they found Patrick. If these changes in Collins became permanent, that is.

"This might be a good time to give you one other thing to hang up," Mrs. Fortini announced, pulling something out of her purse. It was one of those patriotic cloth stars you hang up in your front window, to let people know you have a loved one in the war.

Collins looked at it for a moment, then he actually smiled. "Mrs. Fortini . . . I don't know what to say."

"You could say thank you."

"Thank you," he said and took it from her, then walked

into the living room toward the front window. "I'll put it up right now."

"And Ian," she said. "Notice the color of the star. It's blue, not gold."

"I noticed," he said.

Thirty-Seven

Ezra didn't think he'd ever been this scared. He was making his way down Clifton Ave. now. Most the stores were still closed, either from the holiday or the snow. But there were more people out than he cared to see, all of them white round these parts. Even spotted three policemen in the space of two blocks. Felt like everybody was looking at him much too long, starin' at his belly. Hoped they just thought he was a big fat black man out on some errand. Tried not to look anyone in the eye as they walked by.

Patrick seemed fine under his coat, holding on tight. At one point, he even said, "This is fun." Kids had it so easy that way. He passed the alley beside Hodgins's Grocery. Looked like the boxes were still there just the way he left them. Maybe he should stop back there after dropping Patrick off.

Just up ahead was Bartram Avenue, the road the cemetery was on. Mostly houses on that road, less people. Once he got there, he'd let Patrick pop his head up, see if he knew where he was.

"Almost there, Patrick. I'm turnin' now on that road with the cemetery. Just a few more blocks, son. You doin' just fine."

Katherine couldn't believe the transformation that had taken place in Collins's home over the last few hours. Mrs. Fortini had worked wonders with the things they'd found in the box. A policeman had dropped off a decent-looking tree about thirty minutes ago. Collins had just finished hanging the lights. Quite a few were broken or burned out, but no one cared. She couldn't believe it, but the house was now ready for Christmas Eve.

The only thing missing was a little boy.

Katherine tried not to worry, but it would be dark in a few hours, and there was still no word about Patrick. At the last report, the captain said they had only twelve houses left to check. He'd said something about working on some new leads, but she was sure he said that just to ease their fears.

"Cheer up, Katherine," Mrs. Fortini said. "Don't give up hope."

✑

Ezra was there now, right beside that stone wall. He saw gravestones of all shapes and sizes, as far as the eye could see. Sure enough, no crosses. But plenty of stars. He looked up and down the street. So far so good. Just a few folk down the road a bit. Kids, mostly, making a snow fort. He walked to the first intersection, remembered Patrick saying it was right around the corner. As he got to it, he read the street sign. "Say, Patrick. Chestnut Street, that sound familiar?"

Patrick lifted his head up through the opening. "I think that's it. Can I see?"

Ezra looked around. Couldn't see no harm. "I suppose it's okay to come out now. Let me unbutton my coat." He did, and Patrick slid down his legs like a pole.

As soon as he stood up, Patrick said excitedly, "I think this is it. Right around that corner, that's where Mrs. Fortini lives."

The road hadn't been plowed and didn't look like any cars had come through since the snowfall. "Let me carry you across the street, unless you want to follow behind me."

"I'll follow in your footsteps. I can do that."

Ezra made his way through the snow, eyes looking all about. They made it to the corner; you could only turn right. The sidewalk running the other side of Chestnut looked like it had a path cut through the snow. "Let's cross this street and walk on the other side," Ezra said.

Patrick followed behind him. "I think it's just up ahead, a few more houses."

Ezra froze. "Hold up, son. Uh-oh, this ain't good."

Just up ahead, about four houses down, two big white policemen stepped out from a driveway onto the same sidewalk. Nowhere for Ezra to go. They each took turns looking his way, then started talking, like he didn't matter. Then the first one stopped and looked back at him.

Now he was staring.

Patrick came out from behind his legs. "What's wrong, Mr. Jeffries?"

"Hey, you!" one of them yelled. "Stop right there. Hey . . . there's a boy. He's got a boy, a white boy."

"I gotta git, Patrick." Ezra turned and started to run back toward the cemetery.

"What's wrong?" Patrick yelled. He turned and followed Ezra. "Where we going?"

Still running, Ezra yelled over his shoulder, "Don't follow me, Patrick. You go back now, to your Italian lady's place."

"Stop . . . now! Stop or we'll shoot."

"Don't shoot, you idiot. You might hit the boy."

Ezra turned to see the cops gaining on him, but he didn't see any gun. But Patrick had stopped too. In no time, one of the two cops was on him. He looked so scared. Now they had Patrick, would they still shoot him? He kept running, but his legs were feelin' so heavy and tired.

"Are you Patrick?" the first cop asked. "I got the boy, go after the kidnapper."

"I ain't no kidnapper," Ezra yelled, still running. "I's trying to help the boy." He reached the intersection and looked back just in time to see the fist of the second policeman rise up to meet his face. He collapsed to the ground, and in a flash, the cop was on him. He hit him in the face once more, then spun him over and wrenched his hands behind his back.

"No!" Patrick yelled. "Don't hit him. Mr. Jeffries!"

❧

"Something's going on outside," Katherine said.

"What is it?" asked Collins.

"I don't know," she said as she ran to the window. "The two officers by the driveway are gone. They were yelling something, and now they're gone."

Mrs. Fortini came in from the kitchen. "What? Did they find him?"

"I don't know, but I'm putting on my coat."

Collins didn't answer, just put on his coat.

"Oh, Lord. Let it be him," said Mrs. Fortini.

Katherine was out the door, still buttoning her coat, Collins just a few steps behind her.

❧

"Leave him alone!" Patrick yelled.

The policeman who'd punched Ezra now had him handcuffed and yanked him to his feet by his coat collar. His left eye was already starting to swell.

"I'm tellin' ya, I ain't hurt the boy. I'm the one found him lost in the snow."

"Shut up," the cop said.

The cop holding onto Patrick said, "No, Jack. Let him talk. What do you mean you're the one who found him?"

"I found him . . . in the middle of the storm. Nobody else around to help, so I brought him home. We took care of him, fed him, and now that the snow let up, I brung him home. That's all."

The cop with Patrick said, "Stay here, son, just a minute. Jack, come here."

"He's telling the truth," Patrick said. "He's the one who saved me."

"Okay, kid. Hold on."

The two policemen met in the middle of the street, Patrick and Ezra on opposite sidewalks. "Jack, you hear this kid, right? We bring in this black guy, the story gets out that he saved Patrick, and there goes our reward. You follow?"

Jack nodded. "We gotta let him go."

"And we gotta do it quick. Let me do the talking."

Jack walked over to Ezra. "Okay, maybe we had this wrong, maybe not." He undid his handcuffs. "I'm not gonna arrest you on one condition. You turn around, right now, and go back the way you came."

"You gonna let me go?"

"If you go now."

"Can I say good-bye?"

"No. Go now. Or I take you in."

"Tell Patrick something for me?"

"What?"

"Just tell him Mr. Jeffries says Merry Christmas." Ezra turned and started walking toward the cemetery.

A woman yelled, "Patrick!"

Patrick looked. "Miss Townsend!"

Thirty-Eight

Katherine couldn't believe her eyes. There he was, safe and well. She ran as fast as she dared on the snowy walk, then scooped him up in her arms and hugged him with all her might. Patrick ran just as hard from the opposite direction. The force of their embrace sent them tumbling into the snow. They lay there, covered in snow, laughing, hugging, and crying.

"I've missed you so much," she said. "We've been so worried."

"I was trying to find you, but I got lost in the snow."

They got up and brushed the snow off their faces. Katherine was kneeling so she could see Patrick at eye level, gently resting her hands on his shoulders. "I thought I lost you for good."

"I'm sorry," he said. "I had such a terrible night, and I couldn't stay there anymore. I wanted to call you, but I couldn't find a telephone."

"Oh, Patrick . . ." Tears started running down her cheeks. She realized she couldn't love this little boy any more than if he was her own. She grabbed him and hugged him again.

"Did you hear about my dad?" he said. "They've lost him too."

Katherine pulled back and looked him in the face. "I know, Patrick. I said I would get him back to you as soon as I could. I'm so sorry." She was crying now, but from a different place.

Now he hugged her. "Don't cry, Miss Townsend. It's not your fault. God knows where my daddy is."

Katherine shook her head, trying to get hold of herself. Here Patrick was, after all he'd been through, trying to comfort her.

He gently pulled back from the hug. "Have you met Mr. Jeffries? The man who rescued me?"

"No, where is he?" By this time the two policemen were standing nearby on the same side of the street. Katherine didn't see anyone besides them.

Patrick leaned close to her ear and said, "He's a colored man. He was right here, but the policeman hit him and sent him away. They thought he had done something bad."

At that Katherine stood right up. "Okay, boys. Where is he?"

"Where is who?" one of them said.

"The man who *really* rescued Patrick. He says it was a colored man."

"There was some guy here a minute ago, but he's gone. Look, lady, we've had men out searching for this boy nonstop for two days. What are you trying to do here?"

"I could ask you the same thing." She turned to Patrick. "Is this Mr. Jeffries the one who really brought you home?"

Patrick nodded. "He carried me almost the whole way. And his wife fed me, and his two boys played with me. They were all very nice."

"I think I see what's going on here, gentlemen. And I'm not going to let you get away with it. Which way did he go?"

The policemen looked away, not willing to help.

"Well, I guess it's obvious. He didn't run past me. Patrick, you know where he lives? Think you could find his place?"

"I don't think so."

"Well, you stay right here. He couldn't have gone far. You two, watch him. I'll be right back."

"Hey, lady, c'mon now. Don't do this."

Katherine didn't answer or look back. She retraced the steps already made in the snow along the sidewalk, then across the street till she came to the corner. She turned left at Bartram and picked up another set of footsteps in the snow. Just up ahead, about six houses down, a lone figure walked, shoulders hunched over. He wore a brown overcoat and a knit cap. "Excuse me," she yelled. "Mr. Jeffries?"

The man didn't stop or turn around.

"Please stop. Are you Mr. Jeffries?" she called out. Still he didn't stop. "The man who saved Patrick?" He slowed his steps but didn't stop. "Please, Mr. Jeffries. Please stop. I'm sorry for the way those cops treated you, but his family wants to thank you . . . properly. Patrick wants to thank you too, and at least say good-bye."

At that, he stopped and slowly turned around. In a few moments, she caught up to him. The poor thing, his left eye was swollen shut, and his lip on the right side was split and bleeding. *Can you imagine*, she thought. *To save a little boy's life, take care of him, then go out of your way to bring him home, and this is the thanks you get.* "I can't believe what they did to you. I'm so very sorry."

"The cops said they'd arrest me if I didn't leave right away."

"They'll do no such thing. I'm the lady Patrick was trying to call the night he got lost. I work for Child Services."

"You Miss Townsend?"

"Yes," she said, holding out her hand. "But you can call me Katherine."

He looked at it a moment, then shook it. "I'm Ezra, Ezra Jeffries. Pleased to meet you, ma'am."

"Please call me Katherine." She started walking back toward Chestnut Street, glad to see him join her. "Patrick's grandfather's been worried sick. We'd like to invite you in and hear the whole story."

Ezra stopped. "Ma'am . . . Katherine. I promised Patrick I would get him back to his Italian lady friend. He say the whole reason he left 'cause of how mean his grandfather treat him."

"I know all about that. He was awful, and I don't blame Patrick a bit for wanting to leave. But this thing has changed him somehow. The only thing he seems to want now in life is a chance to make things right with Patrick."

"Really?"

"Yes." They had reached the corner. She looked over, glad to see Patrick still standing there next to the two policemen. Next to the men a squad car had just pulled up. She recognized the police captain sitting inside. One of the men walked over and started talking to him, pointing their way as he spoke.

Ezra Jeffries looked very nervous as he surveyed the scene. "You should know, Ezra, you are entitled to a substantial reward for rescuing Patrick."

He looked startled. "A reward? For helping this boy?"

"I think that's the real reason the police sent you away. You just stick with me, and I'll walk you through this. They won't try to hurt you with me here."

As he stood by the edge of his driveway, taking in the scene down the street, Ian Collins could not stop the tears streaming down his cheeks, and he didn't want to. He wanted to laugh. He wanted to scream. He wanted to shout Patrick's name out loud.

But he did none of these things.

It was Miss Townsend whom Patrick wanted to see, and she was the one, by rights, he should see right now. He stepped back a few feet, just behind a fir tree. Patrick was alive, safe and back home, and that's all that mattered. God had given him a second chance to make things right for Shawn, and Ida, and poor Elizabeth. He was determined not to let anything ruin it.

Miss Townsend would have him back at the house in a few minutes, so he turned around to get things ready. He met Mrs. Fortini halfway, and they hugged. "He looks good. I'm sure he'll want to see you," he said.

"He'll want to see you too, Ian. All you need to do is say you're sorry."

"I plan to, but I want to do it right. Will you bring him inside? I want everything to be just right."

"All right." She hurried down the driveway and turned in Patrick's direction. "Patrick," she yelled. "You're home."

Collins closed the front door and surveyed the scene. He straightened a few things, here and there, but he mostly wanted Patrick to see the wooden soldier. Mrs. Fortini had made a big red bow for it, so he pressed it again to make sure it stuck well to the base. Then he plugged in the Christmas tree lights. He walked over to the radio and turned up the volume. He walked to the coffee table so that it stood between him and the front door, and waited.

He could not recall ever feeling so nervous about anything in all his life.

⌒

They were all walking back to the house now. Patrick was holding onto Mrs. Fortini's hand, just behind them Katherine and Ezra Jeffries. Behind them were the two policemen. The captain had showed up and was driving his car slowly beside them.

The captain had tried to draw Katherine into a debate

about who had a right to the reward, pointing out all he and his men had done, as well as the firemen who'd volunteered. She'd interrupted him and simply said, "That's all a matter for Mr. Collins to decide."

Mrs. Fortini looked down at Patrick and said, "I want to prepare you for something, for seeing your grandfather again."

"Can't I stay with you, Mrs. Fortini? Or Miss Townsend?" He turned to look at her. "You said you'd come get me if I ever needed you. I don't want to go back there."

"I know, I did say that," Katherine said. "And we can talk about that later. But something's happened to your grandfather since you left the other night. He's changed. He's been as worried about you as we were. I think he's really sorry."

He didn't reply.

"And he has a very nice surprise waiting for you at his house," Katherine added.

"He does?"

Katherine nodded. "So is it okay if we visit him first? And if you want after that, you can come home with me, or go to Mrs. Fortini's."

"I guess so."

They turned into the driveway past the fir tree and walked up the steps into the vestibule. "Mr. Collins, may we come in?" Mrs. Fortini yelled through the door.

"You have Patrick with you?"

"Yes, we do," said Katherine. "We told him you have a surprise." She looked down at Patrick. His face was all lit up and smiling. It dawned on Katherine that he was already prepared to forgive this mean old man, even now, before a single word was said.

"Okay, then come in."

Thirty-Nine

The door opened.

Across the room, Collins's eyes instantly locked on the face of his grandson. Tears falling once again. He didn't know what to do, what to say.

Patrick was already smiling, and when their eyes met, he smiled even more. For a moment, neither one moved. He looked down at the wooden soldier, and his eyes got big and wide. "Grandpa, you finished him!" he shouted.

"I did," said Collins. "Merry Christmas."

"For me? He's for me?"

Collins couldn't speak. He could only nod. He held out his arms.

Patrick ran right past the wooden soldier and jumped straight into them. "Thank you, Grandpa, thank you, thank you."

They hugged a few moments more, then Collins gently pulled Patrick back. "Patrick," he said, "can you please forgive a mean old fool? I've treated you so badly, and you didn't deserve it, not any of it. I am so sorry. So very sorry."

Patrick hugged him tightly and held him a moment as he cried, then said, "That's all right, Grandpa. I forgive you."

Katherine and Mrs. Fortini had been watching from the doorway, and now walked the rest of the way into the living room, followed by Ezra Jeffries. "Mr. Collins," Katherine said, wiping her own tears away. "There's someone I'd like you to meet." She guided Ezra to the forefront. "This is Mr. Ezra Jeffries, the man who found Patrick the other night in the middle of the storm. He brought him home to his family, took care of him, then brought him home a few minutes ago."

Just then the two policemen walked in, followed by their captain, in time to hear all this. "Mr. Collins," the captain said, "my men and I have something to say about this."

Ian Collins wiped his eyes with a hankie then looked at Ezra. "Mr. Jeffries, what happened to you?"

"Uh . . . there was a misunderstanding," the captain interrupted. "They thought he was a kidnapper. But about the reward—"

"Please, Captain," said Collins, holding up his hand. "I'm grateful for all you and your men have done, but right now, I want to hear what my grandson has to say. Patrick, would you come here? Please tell us what happened after you . . . after you left the other night, right up until Mr. Jeffries brought you home just now."

Patrick looked around the room. "Don't worry, Patrick," Katherine said. "You're not in any trouble. No one's in trouble. We just want to hear all about your adventure."

He started slowly, but over the next few minutes Patrick told the whole story.

When he was through, Collins walked right up to Ezra Jeffries and held out his hand. "Sir," he said, "I owe you a debt I could never properly repay. But I offered a five-thousand-dollar reward to whoever found Patrick and brought him safely home. I believe, Mr. Jeffries, that money is rightfully yours."

Ezra looked as if he might faint dead away at the news. He was speechless.

"Captain, c'mon now," one of the policemen said.

"Mr. Collins, let's be reasonable here."

Collins held his hand up again. "I'm not through, Captain. You and your men have also sacrificed your time, your safety, even most of your Christmas holiday to search for my grandson. And for that I am also grateful. So, I've decided to give you an additional five thousand dollars to divide among yourselves however you choose."

The captain gasped. "I don't know what to say."

"There's nothing to say. If my grandson was out there to be found, I'm sure your men would have found him. Please take the money and express my thanks to everyone who helped. I've only got one request to make."

"Anything," the captain said.

"Would you personally escort Mr. Jeffries home, so he can spend Christmas Eve with his family, and make sure he gets home safely carrying so much cash."

"I certainly will," the captain said.

"I've got a request of the captain," said Mrs. Fortini.

"What?"

"I'd like Katherine to be able to spend Christmas Eve and have Christmas dinner with us tomorrow. She has no family in town. Could you have someone drive her back to her apartment to pick up a few things and bring her back?"

"Happy to," the captain said.

Forty

It was late afternoon on Christmas Day.

After enjoying a wonderful night of restful sleep and a very pleasant Christmas morning, Ian Collins, Patrick, Mrs. Fortini, and Katherine all sat down to a Christmas feast prepared by Mrs. Fortini. Patrick was sitting next to his grandfather, laughing and talking as if there had never been anything between them but love and affection. If Katherine hadn't seen such things with her own eyes, she would never have believed them possible.

She looked toward the living room at the wooden soldier stationed proudly once more on the coffee table. Except for meals, he hadn't left Patrick's side since the moment his grandfather had given it to him.

Patrick asked her something, and she was just about to turn toward him when she heard a noise outside in the vestibule. Then a shadow appeared in the door window. Then a loud knock.

"Are you expecting anyone?" Mrs. Fortini asked Collins.

"No."

"Did you give the extra reward money to the policemen?"

"They came back for it last night after they dropped off Miss Townsend."

Once again, a knock at the door, a little louder.

"I'll get it," said Patrick. He jumped up and ran to the door before anyone said a word. He opened the door and screamed, "Daddy!"

Mrs. Fortini gasped.

Collins's eyes opened wide, and he dropped his fork.

Katherine looked up. It was almost beyond taking in. How could this be? But she recognized Captain Shawn Collins instantly from his picture.

"I knew God would find you," Patrick said as he buried his face in his father's overcoat.

"I'm sorry if I surprised you," said Shawn as he picked Patrick up in his arms. "I sent two telegrams, but I guess they didn't get through with the storm." Shawn looked down at the wooden soldier on the coffee table. He shook his head slowly back and forth, then looked up at his father, tears welling up in his eyes. For a few moments, no one spoke. "Dad . . . he's beautiful."

"Grandpa made him for me," Patrick announced.

"Did he?"

Ian Collins got up from his chair and all but ran toward his son. "Shawn," he said, erupting in tears. Shawn gently put Patrick down and they embraced, the elder Collins's shoulders now heaving with sobs. "I'm so sorry, Shawn. So very sorry . . . for Elizabeth, for all I've done, all of it. I'm so glad you're alive."

"I love you, Dad," Shawn said, now crying too.

Patrick came beside them both, hugging one leg each.

By now Katherine and Mrs. Fortini had joined in the tears, holding each other up as they watched the scene unfold. After several minutes, Mrs. Fortini said, "So, Shawn, you must be hungry after your long trip."

"I am starving. I haven't eaten all day, just trying to get home."

"Well, you're home now," the elder Collins said, making good use of his already wet hankie. "Mrs. Fortini's made a wonderful Christmas dinner. Come and get some."

As Shawn walked into the living room, he stopped as he passed by Katherine. "I don't believe we've met," he said.

"I'm sorry," said Collins. "Where's my manners?"

"This is Miss Townsend," Patrick blurted out. "She's been taking care of me while we waited for you to come home." And then added, "With Grandpa and Mrs. Fortini too."

"Pleased to meet you," Katherine said, wiping her tears in a handkerchief. "Please, call me Katherine."

"Hello, Katherine. I'm Shawn. Thank you so much for all you've done for Patrick."

"Really, it's been my pleasure," she said, letting go of his hand. "No, that's not enough." She looked down at Patrick. "You have the most remarkable boy I've ever met." She felt the tears about to unleash again.

"Well, I want to hear all about it," he said as they made their way to the table. He picked Patrick up again. "I have missed you so much, my little man."

"I've missed you too, Daddy."

"I hope you're going to tell us about how you made it home," Katherine said. "When you're up to it, I mean. It must be an amazing story. The last thing we heard was a telegram saying you were shot down and missing. Somewhere over Germany."

"I'm really sorry you didn't hear what happened next," Shawn said, taking his seat. "Actually, I've been safe for a couple of days now. After our plane went down, we made it back through enemy lines to England. That's when I found out about . . . about Elizabeth. After that, I caught the first plane home. It's really a long story, and I promise I'll tell you all about it some other time. But tonight . . . tonight I'd rather just think about Christmas." He looked down and said, "I can't believe I made it home for Christmas."

"I know why, Daddy," Patrick said.

"You do?"

"I prayed harder than I ever prayed. And I told God I didn't care if I got anything else for Christmas except you. And look what he did. He gave me you and the only other thing I wanted . . . the wooden soldier Grandpa made."

Forty-One

New Year's Eve, 1943, 10:45 p.m.

Resting on a doily, perched atop a hardwood end table, a General Electric table radio connected the Collins's living room to the big events now underway in New York City. The radio announcer, in that familiar drone, relayed his observations to millions of listeners nationwide. In the background, a big band played a slow dance number.

> The crowd in Times Square is growing by the minute, already numbering in the tens of thousands. The multitude is happy and peaceful, yet somewhat subdued from years past, considering we are a nation at war. And because we are, it's been decided—now for the second year in a row—that the Big Ball will not descend from its post high atop the Times Tower to ring in the New Year. Still, come midnight, we do expect the cheering throngs to scream, the chimes to sound, and church bells to ring throughout the land. But all the while, not far from anyone's mind, will be thoughts of a husband, a son, an uncle, a brother. And for every cheer, two prayers will likely be said. God, keep him safe. God, bring him home.

Shawn Collins looked down at Patrick's angelic face, sound

asleep on his lap, and smiled. Patrick had spent the better part of the day pleading to be allowed to stay up till midnight. Each time he drifted off, Shawn had nudged him, and each time Patrick replied, "I'm not sleeping," and sat right up. This time, though, Shawn knew, he was down for the count. His father had already conceded defeat and went upstairs about thirty minutes ago.

But Shawn didn't mind spending New Year's Eve in this quiet place. He'd take it any day over the fear and terror he'd known and lived in almost every day this past year. He still found it hard to believe he could go to sleep and not worry about waking up to bombs exploding, machine guns firing, and flak cannons going off in his ears. He was glad to just be sitting there not wearing a uniform. Not having every second of his day regimented and on a schedule.

He looked at the radio, then his eyes drifted toward the Christmas tree. His father had agreed to leave it up until tomorrow. Even that, Shawn thought, so unlike him. The change in his father was still holding, one week later. He still didn't understand all that had transpired to bring it about. They hadn't talked anything through yet, but it was clear all the animosity between them was gone. He'd picked up some of the story from Mrs. Fortini and Miss Townsend the day after Christmas; which reminded him, he needed to try and reach Miss Townsend to thank her again for taking such good care of Patrick. One of the most surprising parts of the tale they told was how his father had pulled out all the stops to find Patrick, even paying out ten thousand dollars in reward money.

Shawn smiled . . . another shocker. His father was rich. One might even say . . . filthy rich. Shawn had no idea.

He knew his dad had sold his business when his mother became ill, but he assumed it provided just enough money for him to retire in some comfort. Yesterday, his dad had told him about the deal he'd made with Carlyle Manufacturing and then asked Shawn if early in the new year, he'd meet with his banker and lawyer to sort out his affairs, to "make sure these uppity types aren't robbing me blind." Even before meeting with them, Shawn could do the math in his head. The deal with Carlyle was made before the war. The money had been pouring in ever since, and the interest had just kept compounding.

Shawn thought about this morning. He scratched the last item off his checklist for the week. He got to personally meet with the policemen and firemen who'd searched for his son, and thanked them all for their hard work. But he especially enjoyed meeting and thanking Ezra Jeffries, the black man who'd actually rescued Patrick from the snow and kept him safe until the storm let up. Shawn couldn't imagine how he'd survive if he came home to find he had lost Patrick too.

He smiled as he remembered the look on Patrick's face that morning as they drove up to the Jeffries's apartment. Shawn wasn't sure if he'd ever seen a bigger or brighter smile than what he saw on Ezra Jeffries's face that day. Ezra shook Shawn's hand almost a solid minute and refused to hear anything about what he did for Patrick being anything special. "Just did what anyone do," he'd said. "You do the same for my young'uns." Shawn said that he surely would. Then Ezra brought him upstairs and, while Patrick played with his two boys, told him all about how he and his wife Ruby were going to use the reward money.

First he showed Shawn all the presents under their tree. "Hadn't but one apiece 'fore your daddy gave me all that money." He went on to explain how early in the new year they were going to open up a little corner store and restaurant one block away, specializing in foods colored folks like to eat, food he'd bring up from the South. "Stuff our folks can't get up here no more." Shawn told him it sounded like a wise plan and wished him well.

Just then, Shawn heard a loud bang outside, jarring him from his thoughts.

He tensed up until he heard sounds of laughter and drunken singing. *That's right. It's New Year's Eve . . . not someone trying to kill me.* He looked down, but Patrick didn't bat an eye. How he wished he could have Patrick's outlook on life right now. So simple and secure. They both shared in common the same uncertain future. But Patrick enjoyed such a simple faith, made even stronger now that "God brought his daddy home from the war."

He relaxed a little farther into the couch. The guy on the radio had stopped talking for a bit. Shawn closed his eyes, listened to the music, and stroked Patrick's hair, trying to get in touch with what everyone else seemed to be experiencing. He knew God had certainly brought him home from the war like Patrick said; no other explanation could explain the events that unfolded after his plane had been shot down. But how would God help him face the new year without Elizabeth? Did he even want to try?

But he must. For Patrick, for their future.

God, he prayed, *help me find your will and see the good in all this, to face this new year and find some kind of way to be happy again . . . without her.*

"What, Daddy?"

Shawn looked down to see Patrick's eyes staring up at him. Had he prayed aloud? "It's nothing, Patrick, I was just praying."

"Praying about what?"

"The new year."

"Did I miss it?"

Shawn laughed and rubbed Patrick's head. "No, silly, you didn't miss it."

"Is it midnight?"

Shawn looked up at the clock on the mantel. "Not yet. You awake?"

Patrick sat up. "I think so."

He moved next to Shawn on the couch. Shawn put his arm around him and drew him close. "Then let's go through the new year together."

"I like that idea," said Patrick. "Daddy, I'm so glad you're home."

Dan Walsh is the senior pastor of Sovereign Grace Church in Daytona Beach, Florida, a church he helped found 23 years ago. Walsh lives with his family in the Daytona Beach area. This is his first novel.

Don't miss the sequel to
The Unfinished Gift,
coming June 2010!

The

Homecoming

by DAN WALSH

Revell
a division of Baker Publishing Group
www.RevellBooks.com

Available wherever books are sold.